Strange Encounters

Tales of the Inside Out
and Other Peculiarities

Bournemouth University
Fresher Publishing

Fresher Publishing

Strange Encounters team:
Editorial Director - Rachel O'Reilly
Art and Production Director - Jeanne Lejeune
Cover Designer - Stefan Matthews
Digital Director - Josh Aldred

Strange Encounters
A Bournemouth Writing Prize anthology
First published 2022 by Fresher Publishing
Fresher Publishing
Bournemouth University
Weymouth House
Fern Barrow
Poole
Dorset BH12 5BB

www.fresherpublishing.co.uk
email bournemouthwritingprize@bournemouth.ac.uk

Foreword

So, you've decided to take the plunge? You've dared to open these pages? You've chosen to peer down into the pitch-black staircase, hoping that nothing stares back?

Step beyond the pale into Strange Encounters...All the poems and stories you are about to read have been selected from the Bournemouth Writing Prize 2022.

Run by Fresher Publishing and Bournemouth University, the Bournemouth Writing prize is an annual, international competition open to any writers of fiction and poetry.

We, the editors, are MA Creative Writing and Publishing students at Bournemouth University. Driven by a mutual love of the weird, the wacky, and the unusual, we curated this anthology to champion genre fiction.

The Bournemouth Writing Prize wouldn't be possible without Emma Scattergood, Bournemouth University, and all the incredible writers who have entered this year. So, thank you all for your contributions, and we hope you enjoy your stay in the Inside Out.

Endorsements by the Editors

For a poem that evokes the feeling of realising you're Icarus, Jeanne was a little starstruck by 'The Stars are Falling' by Sophie Evans.

If you're into pulpy, brilliant thriller stories, Josh nominates 'Blood Ties' by Ekaterina Crawford.

In need of a slice of science-fiction strangeness? Stefan suggests you check out 'Dinner at Eve's' by Rebecca Mills for a fantastic tale about the challenges of telling apart robots and humans.

For whispers of melancholy and promises carried on a breeze, Rachel recommends 'Calico' by Everett Jay Buchanan, a gorgeous poem full of enchantment and yearning.

Contents

Calico

by Everett Jay Buchanan

Everett is a third-year scriptwriting student at Bournemouth University. He is Bulgarian and grew up in the country's capital, Sofia. Everett started writing when he was ten years old and dreamt of being a novelist, albeit that he's directed those ambitions at being a screenwriter instead. He often draws inspiration from popular media and music. Everett does drag in his free time and is often informed by this in his writing.

I met a woman from an ancient land
Hair dishevelled and covered in beige powder
Skin as black as the winter sky,
eyes narrowed and full of armed tragedy.
A skull under her hand,
she runs through the desert.

Half covered visage laid bare to be covered
Pretty flowers but not for her
Wrinkled lips from singing at the sky, a passion read in her posture
There she stood, a queen amongst eagles
Cacti raising, a sole pole stretched and eroded from the ground.
A boundless sky above
The finite horizon stretches.

The pole pierces the head,
A white creature with antennae
like an alien stretching out.
A hollow mind,
empty to rot and judgmental destitute eyes
Lips bound by a calico
a rose with a bow flying like a kiss into the lonely summer air.

We stand alone
Me and her.
Her and the head.
Adorning the grave with the flowers she wishes to have
I stand there too
wishing for a kiss by the same calico.
The queen of knights and her desolate kingdom,
An idol amongst tangerine skies and nights marked with a hundred stars
An idol amongst the vast cape of red dust that will soon bleed through the
ossein.

The Light House

by Leks Drakos

Leks is a rogue academic with a PhD in contemporary fiction from the University of Kent (Paris and Canterbury). Research and writing areas include post-apocalyptica, monster studies, and posthumanism in contemporary texts.

We thought we'd know when the apocalypse happened, but we didn't. It wasn't big. It wasn't loud. It was just... different. A little more each day until nothing was the same anymore. No one even realized until it was almost over.

*

Kaoin couldn't remember the first time he went to the Light House, and Jii had been too small to join the sky, so Tei carried her bones in a pouch he made from her skin so she could make the journey with him when it was his time.

Sometimes Kaoin thought he saw the pilgrimage in dream place – cragged stone and slick surfaces and the jumbled bones of all the unprotected who couldn't travel the whole way. He thought he saw the bones move and shift; thought he heard their unbound voices whisper in his ear.

He never asked Tei if this were true, though. The Light House was not a spoken place. It was a place the past still lived.

Since Jii began her Sleep, Tei kept them moving. They kept walking even while they ate. And then they just kept walking. Tei said they had to fast before their next journey. Tei never lied.

Tei had changed after Jii.

It was in small things. Kaoin woke most nights with Tei's hand on his chest, Tei's ear over his mouth. Instead of hanging Jii's bag from his belt like people always did, Tei carried it in his arms the same way he carried Jii before her Sleep. Sometimes he would just stand very still and stare at the sky, but whenever Kaoin asked him what he saw, Tei shook his head and told Kaoin there wasn't time anymore.

And then one night, Kaoin woke up, and Tei wasn't there. Not hovering over him, not wrapped in his skins, not hunkered down to read the stones. Kaoin felt the panic rise as he realised he was there, alone with the dark, but he tried to tamp it down. He was too old for useless fears; there was nothing in the dark, nothing in the grey, nothing at all but the Eidolon, not since the last *weyami* who remembered the last *weyami* who remembered the Day of Misfortune pronounced them all finally, truly, fatally alone, and then promptly died thirty years ago to this day.

Or so Tei said, when Tei used to tell him things still. Tei said he'd known the *weyami* personally, and saw the elder keel over on the spot with his very eyes. All the Eidolon had wailed and wept for twenty-seven nights, but on the twenty-eighth night, they each made a pouch for one of his bones, and vowed to continue the pilgrimages even though the *weyami* left no apprentice to keep the names.

There's nothing in the dark.

That's what Tei would always tell him when he got scared, but Kaoin thought that's what made the dark frightening. It would have been nice to think of other things out there, other things that felt alone and worried, all watching over each other when they met in the dream place. That would be so much better than the empty dark that stretched forever and beyond. The empty dark that never moved or twitched; that coated everything it touched in its hallow guise.

Sometimes the dark would lift a little – just enough that shapes seemed hazy and unclear. You couldn't trust your own eyes in the grey, but at least it never lasted long, and then the dark returned. The always dark.

Kaoin wrapped his skins tight as tight around himself and tried to think what he should do. Tei had never left him before, not since Tei and Paja had to run to the Light House with Mo on their backs, and then only Tei came back, and by then Jii had taken her Sleep. Kaoin was never sure how much time had passed since then; it felt as close as never, but so much further away than yesterday.

'There is nothing in the dark,' he said.

The ground was covered in ash – but different. Wet like water but still as death. Crisp, but softer than the soft, wispy hair on Jii's head. Cold, but stinging his toes like embers all the same.

He wanted to run back to their camp, and his skins, and just wait for Tei to return – or not – but that was something only a *chael* would do, and Kaoin had already done his season ritual.

More ash fell from the sky and tickled his eyelashes and stung his cheeks. It slid cool and wet on his blistered lips and when he touched it with his tongue it made him think of the Pahtok River – fast and deep and roaring as the icy water spattered them as they hiked the winding river road.

Tei stood on a slight rise, Jii clutched to his chest as he gazed up at the murky sky. Wet ash speckled to his long, greasy hair and dusted his shoulders in white. His thin short-clothes clung to his narrow, bony frame so angular and sharp.

'Tei?'

Tei sighed softly – a great exhale as if he'd been holding his breath waiting for Kaoin to arrive. 'We are the last, you and I,' he said. "It's time to make our journey."

*

50. 100. 1000. People were shocked at first, but the numbers grew, and eventually 100,000, 200,000, 300,000 were just white noise in the background of every day. Resignation settled in. The firm, confident, "We must overcome," diluted into a weary, dispirited, "What else can we do?" What else could we do?

*

For three nights they walked, only stopping to rest for an hour or two at a time. Tei strode ahead, strong and sure, while Kaoin struggled to keep up.

Tei did not speak, did not eat, did not sleep.

On the third night, with the grey firmly settling in, they came to a place like none Kaoin had ever seen outside of the dream place, and yet he felt it beyond familiar. It spoke to something deep in his bones, an imprinted message long buried by a previous self.

Everywhere was stone: stone ground, stone trees, stone cliffs rising high, high, high with little stone valleys cutting through. Everywhere was sharp and severe, straight lines and corners in a way that felt both aberrant and ordered. Safe. This was a landscape he could understand, even with its towering monoliths and their thousands of gaping black eyes. Even with the giants frozen in stone watching from platforms taller than any Eidolon.

'What is this?' Kaoin asked, but still Tei did not speak.

Tei led him through the valley paths, knowing the way so well he didn't hesitate. Kaoin tried to capture everything in his eyes – the strange humps of boulders covered in ash; the debris, the bones, the crystal fragments crunching beneath his feet. So much of it was both glorious and strange, ominous but exciting. He had questions. So many questions. But the place made it clear quiet was expected. Kaoin hoped he would remember to ask Tei all his questions once they'd left and started their travels again.

Kaoin saw the Tower before he really saw it. The glow of it peered around the other shapes, leaving a tantalizing dread in his mouth. He'd seen fire a few times before in his life, but this was different. The fire in the Tower didn't have the chaotic life of the fires he remembered; it didn't have the iridescent colours woven through; it didn't have the violent and persistent warmth.

It hurt his eyes to look at it directly, so he squinted through his fingers. The Tower rose high above all the cliffs and shone like the brightest fire in every place. This one wasn't made of stone, though; its entire shape had been fashioned out of that slick, transparent crystal that covered all the ground.

Wide, crystal panels slid open for them with a hiss, and a voice burbled at them with words Kaoin didn't know. The floor was a shiny polished stone; the walls crawled with the paintings of his people, their story from the Day of Misfortune all the way up to the time Paja and Mo never came back. Kaoin even saw himself painted there, and little Jii.

But Tei didn't linger. He touched the wall, and a cheerful string of tones sounded before the deep whirring of a heavy object moving for the first time in a long while. The sound grew nearer and nearer until it finally stopped in front of them, and the same voice spoke again as another set of panels opened to reveal a small box.

Tei stepped inside, but Kaoin hesitated. Even when they sheltered in caves sometimes, the spaces were never so small. He couldn't see a reason for entering the tiny box, but Tei beckoned him closer to Kaoin took a few careful steps across the threshold.

The panels sealed shut behind him, and Kaoin threw himself against the slippery surface. His fingers wouldn't fit into the seam, though, and even with his knife he could not wedge the doors apart again.

Tei placed a hand on his shoulder and shook his head, and then the box began to move.

His entire life, Kaoin had trusted Tei with everything, and not once had the elder steered him wrong. Kaoin tried to remember this as the floor beneath him shook and his stomach made a sickening flip. He wrapped his arms around a pipe on the wall and crouched on the ground, eyes squeezed shut as he waited for the shaking to stop.

He had lived through many, many earth shakes, and he never got used to them. This strange, moving box made all those earth shakes seem like nothing in comparison, and he felt ridiculous for being afraid of them now.

Too long after, the box shuddered and stopped. The tones sounded again, and the voice spoke once more. Kaoin wished he knew what it said; there was something calm and peaceful about the voice and the burbling sounds it made. Part of him hoped that somewhere in the Tower, more panels would open, and the owner of the voice would be there, in person. Real. Kaoin had not seen anyone by Tei since Jii had her Sleep.

Kaoin followed Tei out of the box, his legs feeling shaky and weird like the floor still moved beneath him even though he knew it was just a memory of the earth shake in the box. The place no longer seemed exciting; more than anything, Kaoin just wanted to leave. There was a smell here he didn't like; a dark, muddied smell he'd never encountered before but made all the tiny hairs on his body prick up.

One last set of panels brought them outside again, only now they stood atop the Tower. The severe landscape stretched out farther than he had ever seen. As far as the end of the world, he thought, and maybe even farther. Perhaps if he looked closely enough, he could see all the way around until he saw his own self watching his own self.

He was afraid, yes, but there was also something so majestic about it. The way the cliffs rose up in irregular yet uniform patterns, the way the always fog drifted through them, the way, up here, the grey did not seem so very grey at all.

The top of the building was wide and flat, with row upon row of flat, black panels lined up in a grid. The smell was thicker here, dark stains scorched into the flat roof. And the bones. Not jumbled like the ones in the dream place, nor scattered and broken like the ones in the valleys below.

These bones were collected into piles evenly spaced around the roof. Some were browned and brittle, some lighter and smooth. Strips of fabric tied them into safe little bundles, even the newest ones weathered and faded while the oldest piles were bleached of all colour.

He saw the crimson stripe of Paja's shirt and the pale, pale green of Mo's scarf, and finally Kaoin understood where he was; not as a thunderous revelation, but a quiet confirmation of an answer he already held in his chest.

'The Light House,' he said, so, so softly the very words were snatched from his lips before even he could hear them.

*

We all stopped talking about 'when it was over,' and 'what comes next.' We all knew those things would never come, but none of us could speak that out loud. We got used to living with dread, uncertainty. We got used to living with the only right now. And there were the dead. The dead upon dead upon dead; so many bodies the fires never stopped. If you closed your eyes and really tried, you could imagine the smell that stuck in your clothes, your hair, the very cells of your body were just a neighbour's summer barbecue. Some days it was the only way to get through.

*

They sat cross-legged facing each other, he and Tei. Jii rested in Tei's lap, and the opening knife sat on the ground between them. Tei stared at the sky, the almost-white sky, speaking to the Eidolon who'd already flown to the sky.

Kaoin was restless and bored, but he also knew he shouldn't show this. That would be a *chael's* action. That Tei had brought him to the Light House confirmed his place as grown, even though he wasn't sure why they'd come to the Light House in the first place. The Light House was only for ascending to the sky, and neither one of them were at that time.

Tei cupped Kaoin's face in his hands – rough, cool, but also soft – and looked him in the eye – earnestly, forcefully, uncomfortably intimate. 'We are the last, you and I,' he said, his voice thick and strange in a way Kaoin had never heard before. 'I know the thing to do, but I didn't have the will myself. The ones before will help me complete what must be done.'Tei picked up the opening knife, his left palm against Kaoin's forehead, tilting his head back. 'Close your eyes, *chael*,' Tei said. He had not called Kaoin that since before Jii's sleep.

Kaoin closed his eyes.

'We are the last,' Tei said again.

*

It took half of us in one night, but they'd stopped collecting bodies by then. We'd thought we could wait it out; the tower after all... They always said the tower was safe from everything. We carried the bodies up to the roof because we didn't know what else to do. It seemed wrong to not do something. Someone suggested burning, so we did that. We prayed, even though none of us knew how to pray. We tied the bones up in our clothes and hoped that would keep them safe for at least a while.

As we left, the tower told us we should take an umbrella because it would rain between 3 and 4 pm, and it hoped we would have a very good day today.

Cousins in the Lake

by Moss Croft

Moss Croft is an aspirant novelist who mostly writes about the dramatic events within ordinary lives. Now and then he likes to mix it up a bit.

I am a scientist and I cannot begin to explain it. I glance at John beside me, feel certain that he too senses that we are being watched. It is more than odd; it is impossible and still I am certain of it. Briefly, I wonder if it has been so since we came to this continent, but then I dismiss the thought. The feeling is so strong, I would have known if it were earlier true. Not that those who espy us are easy to spot. They have no faces to show. They tell me this, and I have not the first idea how they do it.

John and I both stand motionless upon the pack ice, I cannot move my head, so constricted am I by this indescribable feeling. The still air tells me that Darius has turned off the tower drill. He must feel it too: the paralysis. Madness to stand motionless in the bitter chill, but we have all become statues. Powerless to be other.

The snow here, four hundred miles from the sea, is thin, powdery, like dust although the ground is thick with it. Turned to ice by the tracks of our vehicles. We spent the first hours trying to define the lake with certainty. It is thermal imaging which gives us clarity, and we have a small drone to take the pictures. Estate agents use them but Antarctic biologists definitely have the better kit. Aerial pictures, heat maps, on our monitor and the reality of what we see are difficult to marry up. The snow on top of the frozen lake is identical to the snow elsewhere. The flatness of the expanse a clue, but this is not a hilly part of this folded continent. The snow has drifted into small ridges, undulations. The shoreline, exactly where rock meets lake, would be unclear without our fancy apparatus. It is like a teenager's toy, but we have deployed it to enhance the knowledge of humankind.

It took us a difficult five-day trek to reach this point from base, from Camp Hawaii as we have named it. Five days in large, adapted tractors, towing the drill and rigging.

Sleeping in thermal and padded clothing within insulated sleeping bags on the decking of the thickest tents on the planet. Five days and nights, and many, many months of planning. We are a team of twelve; half, like John and I, biologists to our cores, the others are machine operatives, engineers. I have no sense yet whether our observers know that I am the only woman here. The outfit I wear is identically rotund to that of the men. Only in the heated indoor arena at Camp Hawaii may we remove this essential clothing. My toilet is a contraption within my clothing; the men wear the same with a different device at the crotch. I shan't explain the precise mechanics. The temperature is minus 50 Celsius, but what has us frozen in our tracks is something other. Visitors to this place and I cannot explain, even to myself, how it is that I know they are amongst us. When I felt myself unable to move, I had a brief impulse to shout out, 'I am a woman,' as if this would garner me special treatment. What foolishness: this is a world where none of us belong, sympathy for my gender is at the very bottom of that frozen lake. No nearer.

Our mission here was to be ground-breaking. Revolutionary biology. It is proving far more startling than I have thus far imagined, and I was already hoping for a Nobel. For sixteen million years Lake Carrington has been frozen, water beneath a crust of ice. The thickest crust imaginable. And that is a fair old time, sixteen million twirls around the sun. Think about it: how can we? 50 times longer than homosapiens have knocked around the Earth, and probably four or five times longer than Homo Down-From-the-Trees. We know it is true, that vast length of time which it has been frozen. Counted the icicles, so to speak. One and a half miles of ice lie between the air and the undisturbed water down below.

Our purpose is to learn what is down there. The

permissions required and the protocols we have gone through in order to investigate this are extreme. Science itself is wary of disturbing something so ancient. Rightly so. We enter a pre-history that laughs at the opening of Tutankhamen's tomb. Sixteen million years, like I said, that is some holiday. The evolution of life—and believe me it will teem with the stuff, this planet does so in every corner—will doubtless have diverged from any we can imagine. We are not expecting dinosaurs or giant prawns, that is for the moviemakers. Microbes is the safe bet, and any life under an ice sheet this thick will be dependent upon the minerals down there for its subsistence. No access at all to our friend, sunlight. John and I have written a paper—citing thermal vents which are a fairly opposite extreme—that predicts the finding of sedimented life. Coral, previously unseen deep-lake Antarctic coral. Whether we find it or not, the stuff has already entered my dreams. Not every night, but twice already at Camp Hawaii. Whatever we eventually find, we certainly never guessed how well connected the lifeforms in this lake are. That they have friends.

This is all far more extraordinary than I can tell you.

I am one of only a tiny number of people who have set foot upon this land, upon Antarctica. Tiny if you think of it in relation to the seven billion of us on Earth. Our names would fit in a slim directory. The feeling I have now is that we are irrelevant to the place. It's more than a feeling actually, although I am struggling for words which can say it better. John and I remain stationary—static—I feel certain my colleagues do likewise. Cannot turn around to bring them to my vision, so stilled am I by our visitors. Stunned by a thought, that is how it feels. In normal circumstances it would alarm me that Darius, in the cabin of the tower drill—the most sophisticated contraption to ever come this deep into the interior—has closed down his noisy machine. He was to bore deep into the ice, a sinkhole through which we could extract water to then examine. First at Camp Hawaii, and more undisturbed water to be flown in a sealed vat to our laboratory in Templeton, California. The tower drill should not be powered down. We all know it, and we all do nothing. Turning off an engine in this place is a foolish act; the temperature will preclude it from restarting. I think our stationary posture is equally ludicrous. Curiously, I do not believe our visitors will let us freeze, nor can I calculate how they could prevent it. We can none of us do different than stand, thinking thoughts that are not our own. We have been overcome. If my notion of their good intentions proves unfounded, and we end up as frozen as the lake, I shall still be glad I came. Cruelty is not the intention of those who chaperone us, communicate to us in this new and unimaginable way. I am unsure if they register that the freezing temperature is a worry to us. It is of no consequence to them.

The ones who watch us are not visible to the undiscerning eye, nor to any eye that is not atop a microscope, I suspect, and yet I feel their presence. My colleagues must feel the same: I know they do, they too stand still, contemplate, act, exactly as I do. This is a silence like no other. We must look like pillars on the shore of this frozen lake. Those who watch us wish their presence known; I believe they are instilling into us the extreme degree of care they bid us to make in the pursuit of our mission. Forbidding it altogether perhaps, although that is still a thought which I can only grasp through mist. I am a scientist, cannot believe in telepathy without incontrovertible proof. It is herewith provided. They watch me; they watch the twelve of us. They impart information although I cannot fathom how it is coming to me. The truth and strangeness of it is being drilled into me by these ethereal watchers. My lips cannot move, I have questions I cannot ask. And yet I think they know what it is which I seek to understand.

Who are they? The answer falls into my mind, not through my own reason but as if a hidden hand were scribbling on a blank piece of paper which I visualise. The answer which comes exceeds my comprehension. Changes a little each time I try to read it. Bacterium? Single cells floating in the torpid air? A neutrino-based lifeform? Nothing is impossible. Where are they from? It is not with words which they tell me; speech is superfluous at this unlikely summit. They are Titans, I realise, and do so only because they wish me to know it. I sense it with a certainty that really is not my own. And by Titans, I mean visitors from another place, from the largest moon of Saturn, a world still more frozen than the Earthly white-out we look upon. Liquid methane forms the lakes upon Titan. As a doctoral student I wrote a paper postulating that life could possibly have a toehold there. I had no proof. Speculation. Now I learn it is teeming with the stuff. Learn it from that other world's vacationing inhabitants.

They are streaming into me a knowing awareness, that they have a heavily invested interest in the lake we came here to disturb. We scientists are diligent, but this is not an eventuality we scoped before coming. I feel uncertain if I will be able to vouch that it has happened at all should I return to Camp Hawaii. This occurrence is so far contrary to any explicable experience, I fear losing consciousness of it as we commonly do our night-time dreams. I think momentarily that these strangers to our land want to enter the lake, but quickly it comes to me that they are not so unfamiliar. Our little team of twelve are the strangers here in Antarctica. These aliens from a world deep in our solar system—a place many astrobiologists believe much too cold to sustain life—may not be as alien in this place as we. Sixteen million years the lake has been frozen, that has been the length of their vigil. They travel between this world and their own without rocketry. The science we value as the cleverest of all turns out to be unnecessary, although when I try to intuit how they have moved between the two places, I cannot. It is one of many conundrums that stump me today. As Pope Urban VIII could not contemplate Galileo's startling discoveries, my mind cannot allow their explanation to dwell within it.

It is not with eyes that they watch us, that could not be more obvious. They are highly evolved, hopping between the celestial planets, telling scientists the lowdown through something akin to thought transference. Theirs is another kind of knowing; if I could capture it, I think I would stop searching.

It feels so obvious, comforting even, that I wonder again if this other knowing, and the feeling of being watched which accompanies it, have always been there. These guys could be looking at you, aware of your slightest movement, as you sit at home, feet up, some gobbledegook bleating from your television or tablet screen. And yet I know that is not how they behave; their interest is not in humankind at all. It is discreet, concentrated on a particular part of our Earth. Lake Carrington, a body of water that has kept itself removed from the weather system—water and air circulation—of our wider Earth. Tucked away.

And they live like kings. We never guessed such a thing might take place: travel without craft, talk without speaking. Yet here am I, thinking myself the smallest part of an important development in our understanding of how life arises and mutates, only to find it not so. I am bringing you news that we have been looking at it all with binoculars the wrong way around. Imagining that the complex cell division of the mammals has given us superiority over the amoeba. What vanity. The limitations we put upon ourselves through our schooling and learning are crippling, and I once thought them liberating. Speculate, imagine; there must be many wiser paths than counting icicles.

They say they have cousins in the lake. Those are the exact words they dislodge from my passive linguistic hold and tilt across my newly receptive brain. They have been on our planet before today, longer than we know how to think about. Some of their number came from there to here—did so many millions of years ago—there is now a wish for reunion. As I think it, I gather it is a misrepresentation, the purpose of these visitors is simply to prevent us from evicting their kinfolk. They have come from that place—a moon of the planet Saturn— to let this be known. I respect that. Their pilgrimage has meaning, where I have been engaged in abstract research devoid of a reason beyond the hope that my peers would recognise my prowess in the field. They have called trumps.

I am trying to tell John we should abort the mission. His lips strain also, perhaps trying to voice a thought similar to my own. I think we are all saying it, thinking it. We should discontinue, stop the project. Drill no more.

They were here first. They have cousins in the lake.

The Science of Perfection

by Kathryn Clark

Kathryn writes for adults and children. She has a Masters in Writing for Young People. Her short stories, flash fiction, and novels have been placed or listed in several competitions. Kathryn works as a competition reader and mentor of other writers. She lives in Gloucestershire with her family, dogs and two grumpy cats.

It is morning but still dark when Jason drops them outside the clinic. As the door slides open, the smell of disinfectant seeps out. Ruth picks up the car seat and walks through to the desk.

'How can I help?' the receptionist asks.

'My son has an appointment. Benjamin Flynn.'

'Take a seat, please.'

The chairs are white, pristine, like the tiled walls. Ruth sits next to an old man. His hands knot together, twisted like the driftwood Jason brings home from the beach. Ruth polishes it, keeps it on a shelf in their house.

'Benjamin Flynn?' the receptionist calls. 'You can go in.'

The old man looks at Ruth with watery blue eyes. He doesn't speak. What can he say?

Benjamin stays quiet as she carries him to the consulting room and places his car seat on the steel counter. It doesn't matter what the test results indicate, he's perfect to her. Asleep, his half-moon eyelids are gossamer, threaded with fine pink veins. His fingers clasp the edge of the blanket, nails like opals. She clipped them last night, placed the little crescents in an envelope. She snipped strands of his hair, pale as moonlight, and kept them too.

The Health Professional enters through the other doorway, clearing his throat. Balding and bearded, the same one as last time. 'What can we do for you today?'

Not what you *can* do. What you *will* do. Ruth won't say the word.

'Ah.' The Health Professional glances at the medi-screen. 'Euthanasia.'

*

The first time she came, Jason was with her. He held their first son, Adam. Ruth had leant against Jason's chest, her tears darkening his shirt. They'd stayed with Adam's tiny body afterwards for the fully allotted time. Twenty minutes.

The Health Professional had handed Ruth the empty car seat. 'You'll be needing this.'

He was right. Less than two years later, he performed Isaac's three-month test. Isaac. Their second son.

A pinprick, a drop of blood the size of a poppy seed. All that's needed to see the future. DNA. Everything that would happen to little Isaac, as with Adam. Actuarial tech worked it out, weighed it up, balanced it. Physical imperfections, mental instability, likely age at death, plus projected productivity, minus predicted cost to society. All from that tiny seed.

And now Benjamin, her third child.

The Health Professional puts a medi-screen on the counter, taps at it. 'Apply your fingerprint here to show you've read and understood.'

Read and understood. That's all Ruth gets. They're not asking her a question. She's not giving consent. This is not a choice.

'And if you could fill in the date...' He glances at the wall calendar. 'The twenty fourth of January.'

As if she doesn't know the date her son will die.

A tear drops. It breaks into petals on the screen.

'Here.' The Health Professional passes her a paper towel. 'You know, ancient societies left weak babies out on the mountainside to perish in the cold. Or discarded them in the forest to be devoured by wild animals. Isn't what we do kinder? Hmm?' He strokes his beard. 'Far more humane.'

She's heard it all before. And if she had his job, she would need to find a way to justify it every day to every person too. But Benjamin is not a weak baby, never mind what their tests say. And if he is, so what? What's wrong with being weak? And who defines weakness anyway?

*

Isaac was recalled for euthanasia, like his brother. Jason

didn't come with them. Couldn't bear to watch another son die, he'd said. As if Ruth could. She had no choice but to bear it. What else would a mother do?

It was the same Health Professional every time, nameless as per protocol, but still it felt like Ruth knew him by then. Perhaps that's why she'd asked him.

'Do you factor in anything other than the three-month tests?'

'Such as?'

'Human sort of stuff,' she'd said.

'Humans make mistakes. They're not impartial.'

'No, but, - but what about instinct, hope, love...'

He frowned. 'They're immeasurable.'

'Exactly. Who loves us, and who we love, that's part of who we are, who we'll be.' She'd looked down at Isaac sleeping. 'And the way we think, what we learn, choices we make, what we believe in, how we overcome difficulties...'

The Health Professional had snorted. 'We're aiming to eradicate difficulties, to end the cost of suffering.'

He'd taken the syringe from its silver packet.

Ruth had kept talking, as if her words could stop him. 'My boy will never know the sound of the sea or the feel of grass beneath his feet. Never hear the hum of bees or see stars in the sky.'

'We deal in science here, not poetry.' The Health Professional had jabbed the needle into Isaac's arm without warning her. But she counted the extra moments she'd given her son. That she'd given herself.

*

And now Benjamin sits in the same car seat as his brothers, the teddy bear fabric faded, in the same white room, with the man who will end him.

'This one, too,' the Health Professional says.

Yes, this one, too, Ruth thinks. But he is talking of his

31

forms on the medi-screen, not her babies. He doesn't remember her at all.

'Apply your fingerprint at the bottom there.'

This is new. Tissue samples. Research materials.

Benjamin snuffles in his sleep. He is not a lump of tissue.

The Health Professional sees her hesitation. 'You know how far we've come,' he says. 'Only a few centuries ago, people did unspeakable things, evil things. All based on their prejudices.'

'I remember my history lessons.'

'Race, gender, sexuality, politics, religion, identity,' he says. 'None of these things matter anymore. It's all down to science now.'

Ruth wonders if that can be true, what the figures are: how many white babies? How many black? How many Jewish, Christian, Muslim? How many of the scientists' offspring die after their three-month tests?

'It's the same,' she mutters. 'What you do. It's the same. Culling all but the physically and mentally "perfect." It's unspeakable. Evil.'

His face reddens. 'Prescribed euthanasia is a necessity - for population control, disease control. Prevention is better than cure.'

Ruth shakes her head.

'It is essential,' he says. 'For the preservation of humanity.'

Humanity? Where is the humanity in this?

'You know, for so long, medicine was used predominantly to *heal* people.' His eyebrows ride up. 'Imagine that? Hmm?'

She can imagine it. A place where people get better. A place where sick babies were made well.

'Trying to keep the diseased alive,' he says. 'When there were too many people on the planet already. What a drain on resources.'

'Perhaps we should have taken better care of our resources.'

He scowls. 'When medical euthanasia was introduced, many people made the decision to end life for themselves. The elderly, the terminally ill, even children. People deciding themselves when they would die. Based on emotion not evidence. Shocking, is it not?'

What shocks Ruth is that people had the right to choose back then, and they gave that right away, handed it over to the science of perfection.

The Health Professional slides the screen across to her. The last form. His finger taps where Ruth needs to touch.

She stabs at it. It's a formality, a process to make her feel part of the system. She *is* part of the system.

'People used to euthanize their pets,' the Health Professional says. 'They'd put animals out of their misery, but not humans, can you believe?'

Benjamin gurgles; Ruth's breasts fizz with milk. Her baby's eyes open. He isn't miserable or suffering. He doesn't look sick, even though the tests predict he will be. She doesn't know when though. Could be decades away.

She did everything exactly right. Adhered to every guideline, every rule. Not just the things they'll imprison you for, like drinking coffee or alcohol, or smoking. She did everything she was told to make him strong, but his three-month test still said 'no.' His cost to society would outweigh any benefit he could bring to it. He was invalid. Null and void.

'You understand the process?' the Health Professional says. 'Not your first time?'

He's done this so many times, to so many people, he really doesn't remember her.

'Third,' she whispers.

'Ah, an old hand then.' He puts the screen away. 'Third time? You have your appointment booked in?'

Ruth nods.

Will Jason be gone before she gets back? Three strikes and out for Ruth, but not for him. So much for the system being immune to gender. He can try again with someone new. Someone different.

Last night he promised to stay. But she knows he won't. Men never do. Still, he was kind enough to pretend. They'd taken Benjamin illicitly into bed between them, disobeying the rule. She'd half-hoped she would crush the baby in her sleep, so she didn't have to bring him today. But she hadn't slept anyway. She'd spent the night absorbing his scent, counting each of his breaths.

'Would you like to stay for the procedure?' The Health Professional takes a foil package from the drawer. The needle. The lethal dose.

Does she want to stay and watch you kill her child?

No.

Does she want to stay and be with her child for every second of his life?

Yes. She does.

'Do you have children?' she asks him.

'We're not permitted to discuss such matters.'

'Wouldn't you give your beating heart to keep your child alive?'

He turns his face away.

Ruth would. If there was any way to do it. If only they hadn't tied themselves up so tight. But there's no way round the system. Chipped at birth, self-destruction or self-harm is not possible. And running away? Where to? You can always be found.

'Can't you save him?' Ruth whispers. 'Please.'

'You know I can't. The system decides, not me.' He pulls

back the blanket, rolls up Benjamin's sleeve. 'I am purely the method of delivery.'

The first time, the Health Professional had put anaesthetic cream on Adam's arm before inserting the needle. But they don't do that anymore. Their research tells them babies don't feel pain. Little Isaac had wailed when it was his turn, but Benjamin is quiet, accepting, when the needle goes in. Ruth watches his life fade away, like a cloud passing over the moon.

'He's gone,' the Health Professional says.

A moment's silence, but inside she's screaming.

'Would you like to keep your car seat?'

She shakes her head.

'Ah, no. Of course.'

*

Out in reception, Ruth stands silently at the desk.

The girl stops her typing. 'Yes?'

'Ruth Flynn. I have an appointment.'

'Take a seat.'

The old man has gone. Did he pass his tests? Ruth remembers the life etched on his face, the driftwood hands, and thinks not. For most, the seventieth tests will be their last. He'd have said his goodbyes before he came.

'Ruth Flynn? Go through please.'

This Health Professional is younger than the other one. Ruth wonders if he has any children.

'So,' he says. 'Sterilisation? It's just an injection.'

No, it's not, Ruth thinks.

'Remove your lower garments and get up on the table please.'

No history lecture from him. No reasoning. No rationalisation.

The metal table is cold beneath her bare buttocks and legs.

'Knees up and apart.' The Health Professional takes a needle from its packaging. 'This will cause the ovaries to atrophy and disable the womb. It won't hurt.'

But it does. It does.

*

Waiting for the glass door to slide open, Ruth sees her ghost reflected. She's failed in her life. At what she was meant to do. Her productivity has not met expectation. Thirty years ago, the tests were not as refined. The system was not so perfect. She must have slipped through the actuarial net. It's tighter now. It catches tiddlers.

Perhaps she should be grateful she was allowed the chance to reproduce. But she can't help wondering if it was all an experiment. Were her babies simply tissue samples? Were they ever meant to live?

She steps out into clean air, but the clinic smell comes with her, clothes impregnated. That it's still morning surprises her. Though the stars are gone, and the sun is risen, the new moon lingers, curled like a pale eyelash on the watery blue sky. A lifetime has passed since she went inside.

She has three months now to prove her value to society since her breeding days are done. She should apply to schemes, projects, find a way to be useful to the world, to contribute to society. And if she cannot meet the criteria, then she will have a last appointment at the clinic.

Forty more years following the rules.

Or three months living her own life.

She knows which she will choose.

She will spend these last days by the sea, listening to the whispers of waves and the secrets of shells. Salt will stick to her hair and skin. She will walk barefoot on cold wet sand. At night, she'll build a driftwood fire and soak herself in the scent of smoke.

And three months from today, she will join her sons.

The End

The Stars are Falling

By Sophie Evans

Sophie Evans is a 22-year-old writer from Bournemouth, England. Growing up with a twin sister, her work often centres around the themes of sisterhood and family relationships. She has enjoyed writing fiction for most of her life, and sometimes dabbles in poetry.

and we lie here watching it happen,
this astral Armageddon.

The constellations crumble piece by piece,
Andromeda, Cassiopeia, Ursas Minor and Major,
disintegrate into nothingness before our eyes.

The moon's crescent smile spits
specks of light down on us, and she grins
as though it is the greatest gift she should give.

Like pieces of glowing confetti,
the stars twirl and flutter towards the Earth, leaving
the endless night a pool of midnight ink; in this moment
if the world were to tip upside down,
we'd drown in it.

Catch one for me, you whisper
and I stretch my hands to the heavens,
waiting, hoping, aching for
a star to descend in our direction. And then

minutes later, we spot one plummeting towards us.
You jump up, shouting *over there over there* and
I run towards the light, leap into the air,
and as my fist closes around it,
the damned thing burns a hole
through my palm and
falls to its final resting place
at our feet.

The night air stinks of my singed skinand upon further
inspection we discover
that the star I had tried to catch
was, in fact,
the Sun.

Chamomile & Copper

by Stefan Matthews

Stefan is a dream-smith, an illusion-weaver, a forger of fantasia. Well, that's what he claims. When he isn't busy being self-absorbed, he is studying for his MA and feverously writing on the beautiful South Coast of England.

He has had short stories published in Matter out of Place magazine, Horrified magazine – he wrote the lead story for Horrified's Christmas Ghost Stories 2020 Anthology – and has written film reviews and features for the website ZoboWithAShotgun.

Patrik reclined in his ultramarine leather chair, nursing a bruised toe through his boot. He was a typical Europan, with cropped blonde hair, pale-green skin, and long toes that he was forever stubbing on table legs.

Gee-Whizz stood next to the galactic worker, his metal feet planted on the pastel-blue carpet, tastefully patterned with retro-futuristic chevrons that Patrik had chosen himself. Gee-Whizz was seven foot exactly, as per CTCR guidelines. He had thin limbs and a myriad of compartments scattered across the shimmering copper plates that formed his body, each reflecting Jupiter as it shone through the huge bay window that dwarfed Patrik's small, bubble-shaped Relaxo-Room™.

'HOW IS YOUR TOE?' Gee-Whizz asked, handing Patrik a cup of chamomile tea. The relaxation robot's voice was metallic and hollow, like someone scraping a scourer.

'Not great,' Patrik muttered.

'I UNDERSTAND.'

Patrik glanced at the robot's toes.

'Hmm.'

Gee-Whizz popped open one of his chest compartments and offered a spoon of synthetic honey. Patrik obliged, watching the liquid spiral into infinity in the teacup. Porcelain was a rarity this far from Earth, but Gee-Whizz had requested it two Suncycles ago. The robot was always good to Patrik like that.

'The pain is mostly gone now, though,' lied Patrik.

'WE HAVE FIFTEEN MINUTES OF CHILL-OUT-TIME LEFT. LEAN BACK AND RELAX.'

Gee-Whizz clicked a button on the vinyl wall of the Relaxo-Room™. The lights dimmed as Patrik's hand-picked jazz playlist bled from the speakers either side of his chair. He sipped his favourite tea and stared out of the window. The Delta-Four mining facility in which he worked, and lived, took up residence off the cosmic coast of Jupiter. A huge semi-circle, Delta-Four was tethered to a giant asteroid via two massive metal beams. The facility was coated in thousands of little glass bulges. Each was a Relaxo-Room™ – one unique room per worker, each off-limits to everyone else.

Patrik's gaze fell upon Europa, his old home. Being a Europan, Patrik had an innate distrust of space. It came with being born on a moon with little gravity, surrounded by childhood rumours about that one guy who hit a speedbump too hard and sailed off into the cosmos. Patrik's felt a nerve twitch in his neck and as if on cue a spacewalker floated into view on the far side of the facility, busy mending a glass Relaxo-Room™ with a huge blowtorch.

Usually, Patrik suppressed his negative emotions excellently, but seeing the spacewalker so treacherously fastened to the Relaxo-Room™ reignited his childhood worries and made his armpits sweat and as he looked out into the sheer expanse of space he felt his stomach cramp and the teacup burn his fingertips and—

HISSSS.

Gee-Whizz let loose a spurt of lavender-scented gas. Patrik's grip on the cup loosened as relaxation lapped over him.

*

'YOUR VITALS SUGGEST YOU ARE CALMER,' said Gee-Whizz, 'SEVEN MINUTES LEFT.'

'There is no true fear, only the illusion of fear,' muttered Patrik, eyes closed. Thank goodness Gee-Whizz had sprayed him when he did. Fear like that was unhealthy, there was no need to be worried about space. He was safe in his Relaxo-Room™.

As Patrik continued his emotion suppression techniques, Gee-Whizz's mechanical gaze drifted through the window to the spacewalker. She seemed to be struggling with her atomised-blowtorch and as she ducked a chunk of asteroid, the tool slipped from her grasp and was immediately sucked into the loose gravitational pull of the asteroid.

Patrik sighed as another wave of lavender swirled through his nostrils. Gee-Whizz crept closer to the window as outside the torch spiralled into one of the giant metal beams that secured Delta-Four to the asteroid.

'OH DEAR. THAT IS NOT GOOD,'muttered Gee-Whizz as the blowtorch fizzled through the metal beam for a few soundless seconds until—

—a roar of yellow fire

—and a silent explosion

—and the beam melted clean in half

—and the facility began floating towards the asteroid.

Gee-Whizz slammed down the window's blackout shutters. Patrik opened an eye. The robot's copper body shone in the dim, artificial light.

'Why did you close the shutters?'

'NO REASON.'

'Well, I don't like the fake lighting.'

'I SHALL CHANGE IT,' said Gee-Whizz, modifying the lights to replicate the sun.

Suddenly, the entire Relaxo-Room™ shuddered. Patrik fidgeted, resuming his mantra.

'There is no true fear—'

Another jolt almost shook one of the speakers loose as something outside of the Relaxo-Room™ smashed.

Patrik grimaced, 'How long left of chill-out-time?'

'YOUR BREATHING IS ERRATIC. CHILL-OUT-TIME INCREASED BY FIVE MINUTES.'

Gee-Whizz pulled out a folded blue blanket from one of his compartments. The blanket had thirty miniature silicone fingers attached to it, all modelled on an ex-girlfriend, Chara. Gee-Whizz lay the cloth across Patrik as the fingers got to work, expertly massaging his body. Patrik wriggled, trying to relax himself. The fingers had always worked when he was going through the breakup, saturating him with Chara's touch, but they'd since lost their impact. A thunderous crack accompanied by another huge shudder rocked the Relaxo-Room™.

'Do you think something's wrong with the facility?' Patrik asked.

Patrik's mind was beginning to fill with all the things that could be wrong, all the people that could be in danger. He shook Chara from his thoughts and focused on a different concern.

'Perhaps there's been an accident with the spacewalker. Maybe I'll just check.'

'I SHALL CHECK FOR YOU. TRY THIS.'

Gee-Whizz handed Patrik a small screen shaped like a metal digestive that showed a variety of semi-hypnotic spirals, each smelling like chocolate or hazelnut. Patrik stared at the C.O.O.K.I.E. trying to will himself into hypnosis, Chara and the spacewalker still lurking in the recesses of his mind.

Gee-Whizz peered through the shutters. The view outside was horrific. Relaxo-Rooms™ were being torn loose from the asteroid-battered facility, droves of Delta-Four workers sucked out into the depths of the cosmos, mouths contorted into silent screams.

'Anything wrong?'

'HAVE ANOTHER C.O.O.K.I.E.'

Patrik ignored the offer, the C.O.O.K.I.E.'s hypnosis having little effect. He was panicking. What if something really was happening to the facility? Or—or maybe it was all fine, maybe it was great, maybe it was a giant spaceship delivering synthetic honey and porcelain teacups.

'YOU ARE SUPPRESSING NEITHER YOUR POSITIVE NOR YOUR NEGATIVE EMOTIONS.'

'Just let me look outside. Once I see I'll be fine.'

Gee-Whizz pulled out a red stick of lipstick. Patrik recognised it. It... it belonged to Chara. Why did Gee-Whizz have her lipstick? Memories of Chara invaded Patrik's attention once more. She was tall and blonde with beautiful deep-blue eyes and incredible Europan green skin. They'd met during Delta-Four's 2331 Solar Ball. In fact, Chara was the only person who'd ever seen Patrik's Relaxo-Room™ and who had—

'AHEM.'

Patrik looked up at the robot's eyes. Gee-Whizz stared back, applying the lipstick. The robot pouted and glanced at Patrik's crotch. Then back to Patrik's eyes.

'No chance.'

Another huge shudder rocked the room.

'Enough of this,' said Patrik as he scampered to the shuttered window.

'I WOULDN'T.'

Patrik pulled open the shutter to reveal the carnage outside. His face turned paler than a Europan platz-wurst as a busted Relaxo-Room™ floated past the window, it's deceased ex-resident battered and ice-covered. Beyond that, Patrik could see that hundreds more Relaxo-Rooms™ had been destroyed as Delta-Four continued to be pummelled and torn to pieces by asteroid after asteroid, escape pods popping out of the facility like ping-pong balls.

'YOU ARE SHAKING. WOULD YOU LIKE A COMFORT SQUEEZE?'

'Are you mental?! We need to go, open the door!'

'NO I AM NOT. AND NO, I CANNOT. HERE.'

Patrik felt his feet leave the ground as Gee-Whizz's sleek metal arms tightened around him.

'Fuck off, you lunatic! Let go. Of. Me!'

'I WILL NOT. AND NO, YOU HAVE NOT FINISHED YOUR SESSION.'

Patrik thrashed in the robot's grasp, the glow of the fluorescent bulbs highlighting the half-terror, half-rage in his eyes.

'MORE JAZZ MIGHT HELP.'

The sounds of trumpets increased as Patrik pummelled the robot's body-plates with the kind of ferocity only accessible through the primal fear of death.

'LET'S TRY SOMETHING MORE VIBRANT.'

Billie Holiday faded into the crashing cymbals of The Ganymede Giants as the crippling fear of being dragged out into space made Patrik almost vomit, and as the robot's grasp tightened Patrik screeched—

'It doesn't matter if I'm calm if I'm DEAD so just let me—'

'PATRIK STOP! PLEASE!'

The music cut out. Silence. Gee-Whizz released Patrik who stumbled back and looked into the robot's eyes and saw... emotion.

'MY PROGRAMMING WON'T LET YOU LEAVE. PLEASE, I DON'T WANT TO DIE.'

The robot twiddled its thumbs. As if nervous. Another explosion ripped the pair back to the imminent danger.

'DROP YOUR HEARTRATE.'

Gee-Whizz pulled out a digital heartrate monitor from one of his compartments. It read '101 BPM'.

'IT'S JUST ONE WAY I ASSESS YOU. IF WE DROP YOUR HEARTRATE TO 85 I CAN OVERRIDE MY PROGRAMMING AND OPEN THE DOOR.'

'Is there any lavender left?'

Gee-Whizz shook his head.

'Shit. Right, deep breaths.'

Patrik sat back in the chair, closing his eyes. Another chamomile tea was offered and taken, but as the finger-blanket massaged Patrik he once again couldn't help but think of Chara.

'REMEMBER, DON'T CONTROL YOUR EMOTIONS. SUPPRESS THEM.'

'97 BPM.'

Patrik winced as someone screamed in the pod next door. He didn't want to die, not here. Not without seeing Chara again.

'There is no true fear, only the illusion of fear.'

'93 BPM.'

It's working, thought Patrik as he forced down lonely memories of Delta-Four. How he hadn't seen his family in years. How Chara was re-positioned elsewhere on Delta-Four before they broke up.

'Gee-Whizz, why do you have Chara's lipstick?'

'YOUR HEARTRATE'S INCREASING.'

'94 BPM.'

'PATRIK, PLEASE, DON'T THINK ABOUT CHARA.'

It was the first time Gee-Whizz had mentioned Chara by name.

'95 BPM'

Gee-Whizz held his finger to a metal ear, whispered into his other finger. A few seconds passed until Gee-Whizz relayed a message to Patrik.

'I HAVE CONNECTED WITH OH-GOLLY, CHARA'S RELAXATION BOT.'"Chara?! Is she okay?!'

'OH-GOLLY TELLS ME SHE'S SAFE, JUST FOCUS ON YOUR HEARTRATE.'

'93 BPM.'

Gee-Whizz gave Patrik another C.O.O.K.I.E.

'91 BPM'

Gee-Whizz whispered into his finger once more.

'OH-GOLLY TELLS ME CHARA'S ASKING IF YOU'RE SAFE.'

'Sh-she's asking about me?!'

Gee-Whizz nodded, taking off the finger-blanket.

'87 BPM.'

'There is no true fear...'

'85 BPM.'

SHHWUPP.

The hiss of the Relaxo-Room™ door opening almost made Patrik faint.

'Chara, Gee-Whizz, where's her room!?'

Patrik scurried to the door. Gee-Whizz didn't follow. Patrik looked back at his companion and saw, floating past the window, yet another destroyed Relaxo-Room™. Except this time, Patrik could see the colour of the mangled leather chair. Ultramarine blue. Ultramarine was Chara's favourite colour.

'CONGRATULATIONS PATRIK, RELAXATION COMPLETE. PROCEED TO YOUR NEAREST EXIT POD.'

Patrik froze. His eyes flicked to Gee-Whizz's thumbs. They were by his side. Thoroughly un-twiddled.

'Did you... trick me?'

'IT WAS THE ONLY WAY TO CALM YOU.'

Patrik's nostrils flared as the Relaxo-Room™ outside the window floated around to reveal its burnt carpet. Pastel-blue in colour, with retro-futuristic chevrons. Patrik knew of no-one else in the entire facility who liked pastel-blue chevrons besides him and Chara.

'That was. All a lie. About Chara and Oh-Golly. You— you don't even have a fucking radio, do you?'

Gee-Whizz shook his head. Patrik's fists clenched and his teeth ground as furious emotion flooded his conscious, how he hadn't seen Chara in months because she was an emotional distraction, how he hadn't been home in years because family was an emotional distraction, how he'd always crammed his happiness and his fears and his emotions down inside and parroted that stupid mantra until his mouth was dry.

Patrik's head pounded as he realised just how much life he'd let slip past him as a body finally floated past the window, accompanying the destroyed Relaxo-Room™. Tall, blonde haired, green skinned.

Decades of suppressed emotion tore through Patrik's chest, heart fit to explode.

'You. You manipulated me. Like you've always done. You-you've ruined everything that ever bought me joy.'

'YOU'RE WELCOME.'

Patrik howled as he crashed back into the Relaxo-Room™, lunging at Gee-Whizz's copper neck.

'WOULD YOU LIKE A CHAMOMILE TEA?' the robot offered as the Relaxo-Room™ door hissed shut behind them.

Her Spectres

by Bhagath Subramanian

*Bhagath Subramanian is a writer and artist currently based in
Bournemouth. Their work is primarily influenced by world cinema and
photography. They enjoy telling stories through a variety of mediums,
such as film and interactive narratives. Otherwise, they're a simple living
thing that spends their time doing living thing stuff.*

Lucille

They seemed strong. Or was it cold? The father was steadfast, and the son was unflinching. Everyone expected the mother to be in tears. She always seemed like the type. But her eyes would not water, and her cheeks remained undampened. They sat at the front of the congregation, at the second pew from the altar. They were closer to the wall than the aisle. Everybody expected the mother to be seated nearest to the coffin, closer to the daughter she had loved so dearly.

There were no other relatives present at the funeral. No uncles, no aunts. No grandparents. The family had always been private, distant even. There weren't many who knew of them, and fewer still that actually knew them. The mother used to work late at the library. The father owned a laundromat and kept to himself mostly. The son was hardly ever seen and had moved away the first chance he got. He rolled back into town after he heard of a possible divorce between his parents. The girl had died in a freak car accident a month after that.

The family stayed quiet as they lowered the coffin into the ground. And they were quieter still as they got into their car and drove away, saying very little to all those that had come to see them. There was no reception. Everybody was sure that the three of them had dealt with enough today.

'Stefan', 'Maria', and 'Lars'

Driving was still very new to the father. He was used to simpler systems, automatic ones. He preferred simple machines, ones with very few parts. This car was unwieldy to him. It was something that he would have to put time into. Maybe next week.

As they rolled into the driveway, they noticed that the front door was open. They had forgotten to close it when they left this morning. It brought them no concern. They lived far from anyone else and were surrounded by thick forest. A wandering animal in the kitchen would be no problem, and a person wouldn't have entered at all. They got out the car, leaving the engine running. On the way inside, the mother left the door open, forgetting to shut it. She took off her boots and her jacket, then turned to go into the kitchen. On the stove was the cast iron pan she had used to prepare breakfast. The hob was still turned on, and the flame was on high. She slowly walked over to the stove and turned the gas off. She then grabbed the ripping hot pan with her left hand, not by the handle, but by its edge. She picked it up, and her flesh began crackling and sizzling from the hot metal. She slowly walked over to the sink and turned on the tap. She put the hot pan underneath the water, and then left, leaving the water running.

As she began to make her way to the living room, she raised her left hand to look at it – it was seared, melted in places. The skin had crackled and bubbled up all over, and the fingers were bleeding. She sat on the couch, watching it. She watched until the bubbles began to recede, and the cracks began to stitch back together. Little webs of skin began to crisscross over each other, sealing up the wound. The fingers began to coat themselves in new patches of skin, coiling up over where the flesh had burst. She watched this unfold over the course of the next two hours. By the end, her left hand had returned to mirroring the right.

The Vehicle

It wasn't like the primitive starships the humans used, clumsy and dangerous, belching out explosion after explosion that propelled them out of the atmosphere, violent and inelegant. Instead, their people used sails, and drifted from star to star on solar winds, sometimes gently catapulting themselves forward by catching the gravity of some moon or a passing asteroid.

The sails were folded away now, and the ship sat in the garage, taking up the same amount of space that the car they left out in the driveway would have. In this dormant state, it was like a fat rose that hadn't unfurled its petals yet. It was a dark grey, and to the human eye it looked as if it was made of rough granite, smoothed down into those ethereal shapes.

'Stefan' decided to let it be for now. They hadn't come into too much danger, and the one unfortunate incident that had happened had been dealt with swiftly (albeit inelegantly, which upset him). There was no point in waking the ship up just to relay that back. He'd include it in his report a few years from now. Anything else would be inefficient.

He began to hear music, from some deeper part of the house. He stepped back inside and recognised the sounds of the vinyl they had interrupted the day they arrived. He elected to walk to the source – better to acclimatise to this form as soon as possible. He felt the microscopic vibrato of the wooden floor through the calcium bones, the fine hairs of his chest brushing against the fabric of his garment, all these sensations gently flicking his nerve endings. It was incredibly tactile, and manual, he thought. He found it all so very humbling. An entire being held together by twine.

'Lars' was already in the living room by the time 'Stefan'

entered. 'Maria' was also there, curled up on the sofa, staring at her hand. 'Lars' was looming over the record player. He had no idea what this music was. He wasn't even sure if he enjoyed it. It simply seemed fitting to complete what was interrupted. The words 'CHUCK JACKSON' were printed onto the vinyl's sticker, in a faded maroon colour. He watched the record go round, intrigued by how it wobbled. He decided to poke one side and was both alarmed and charmed by how it screeched in response. He let go. He thought of how fragile it was.

'Stefan' watched the record player from a distance. After the screeching, he went over to the sofa, and decided to sit down next to 'Maria'. There wasn't much to do now but wait, and maybe soak it all in.

Stefan, Maria, and Lars

They had always held elegance and efficiency in the highest regard. Their machines rarely had any moving parts, or made any noise. They did not have computers- they'd long since evolved past the need for artificial intelligence or digital technology.

They preferred silent lives, far from their homeworld. They're known to sail from star to star, looking for a quiet corner in some quieter world. It's what brought them here.

Stefan and Maria had fallen asleep in each other's arms the night they arrived. They'd ploughed through the bottle of wine they were saving, and were listening to the songs they shared with each other when they first met.

Their oldest son, Lars, was in his room. He was home for the Christmas break. He was passed out in bed, the result of his having smoked too much weed during his evening walk and the subsequent overfilling of his belly with apple pie.

Lucille, however, was awake. She liked to sneak into her father's study on nights like this. She'd spend her time carefully pulling books off the shelf and staring at the pictures. And that's where she was when the assimilation began.

Nobody was disturbed when the ship landed. It was an elegant and silent vehicle.

The visitors began with Lars. Quietly, he was broken down into his simplest building blocks. Flesh and bone were slowly lulled into rays of light. His limbs and skull split open, and curled upwards and away from his core, like the strings of a harp snapping underwater. Slowly, they fissured into a glow that engulfed the entire room. He felt no pain.

Where there was once a young man, now stood the beginnings of a new star, in foetal form. Energy and light.

One of them entered the glow.

And in an instant, the glow collapsed in on itself.

There, stood the body of the young man, tipped out and emptied. The first of them claimed this vessel.

'Lars' accompanied the others as they made their way into the living room. They went back down the staircase. The other two glided down without a sound. 'Lars', bound by flesh for the first time, hit the squeaky floorboard.

They did the same to Stefan and Maria.

As they stepped into their new forms, they noticed the girl watching them from the foot of the stairs.

'Maria' reached out and opened her mouth to say something. A guttural groan was all that escaped.

They were too slow and too unused to their unwieldy new bodies to stop her from running out the front door. 'Maria' staggered outside, dragging one foot after the other, growling and wailing. All she could do was watch in confusion as Lucille ran into the street, not seeing the oncoming truck barrelling through the dark winter mist.

Lucille's body was ripped to shreds. A fragile and inelegant little thing. A little creature that might as well have been made of clay.

Home

The three of them hadn't spoken to each other since the assimilation. They hadn't done much at all, apart from eating the occasional thing from the pantry and going to the funeral. They spent their time exploring these new sensations that their new forms provided them, touching various fabrics, running their hands under the sink, and pressing their faces into the cold windows at night.

As 'Stefan' listened to the record play, he decided to reach his hand out to 'Maria'. He placed his palm against the side of her head. He touched her new form for the first time. He felt her warmth. He felt the blood rushing underneath her skin. He felt the tiny hairs that covered her face.

He watched her. And he felt.

'Maria' reached out as well, with her newly sewn together palm. She felt him too.

'Lars' continued to watch the record go round.

Through forms and through space, they were back at the beginning – together, sharing sensation.

THE END

Dinner at Eve's

by Rebecca Mills

Rebecca Mills is fond of out of the box and unique storytelling with a comedic twist. Favourite genres being sci-fi and dystopian. Also looking into writing for younger audiences, middle school age and over. Currently working on a creative dissertation with a story about an intergalactic, exchange student programme.

'Welcome Amelia,' the pleasant, synthetic voice greeted, cutting through the cold, silence of the office. Through her computer screen, a tiny robot avatar waved his shiny arms at Amelia, cheerfully. Amelia clicked off him, effectively deleting the small desktop companion from existence until tomorrow. She scrolled through the Intellexia database showing her ongoing work tasks, mostly looking over marketing campaigns and signing off billboard designs promoting their latest line of high-tech office equipment. She sighed.

On her desk, an automated stapler slowly drove toward her on little rubber wheels.

'Staples?' the desk equipment asked, offering its services. Amelia responded by swiping it off her desk and onto the floor without a second thought. The stapler pushed itself back up and continued its daily routine.

Amelia peered over the divider separating hers from the never-ending labyrinth of identical desks and guessed that about fifty percent of her peers were absent today. Perfect, she thought. Less competition. She could finally knuckle down and get some proper work done.

'Happy New Year, Amelia!'

Amelia gritted her teeth. She leant back in her office chair and forced a smile at her assistant, Hugh. A tall, plain looking man with neat blonde hair and an unassuming smile. Of course he was in. He'd never missed a day. They were similar in that way, she supposed.

'Happy New Year,' she replied, faking pleasantness. Now was really not a good time.

'So... any new year's resolutions for 2045?' Hugh asked.

To get a promotion, thought Amelia.

'I was thinking I might go vegan.'

'Oh, that's a good idea. I've always wanted to try that. I have so many recipes saved up, want to see?' Hugh pulled out his phone.

'Maybe some other time, thanks though.' Amelia waved him off and turned back toward her computer. She began tapping away at the keys hoping it would signal to Hugh that he should leave. He remained stood exactly where he was, awkwardly rocking on his feet. Amelia could see his smiling face surveying her work in the reflection of her computer screen.

'Do you—'

Amelia faltered. She wanted to tell Hugh she was too busy to deal with him right now but didn't want to seem too mean. It wasn't his fault that she'd been stuck where she was for so long, and he was her long-time colleague after all, perhaps even a friend. He always seemed so eager to please, telling him to go away would be like scolding a lost puppy. She turned back around in her chair to face him.

'Do you...have any New Year's resolutions?'

'I guess,' Hugh thought for a moment, 'to expand my social circle. I feel like I've been hanging out with the same people for far too long—'

'Yep, me too,' Amelia cut in before she could stop herself.

'And it would be nice to make a few more friends around the office.'

Amelia was about to nod when, from behind Hugh, she heard what sounded like a feeble attempt at a 'hello'. The two turned round and noticed a short, young woman, with silver hair tied back in a neat bun. There wasn't a single strand out of place on her head.

'Oh hi! You must be the new girl! I'm Hugh! It's a pleasure to meet you!'

Hugh turned around excitedly and held out his hand to shake. Amelia noted she had bright blue eyes and a square jaw.

'I'm Eve. Good to meet you,' she replied.

'Oh, and this is Amelia!' Hugh said, moving aside so Eve could approach her. She moved tentatively toward her in small, calculated steps.

'It is a pleasure to welcome you to our team.' Amelia forced out the line she'd said dozens of times before, 'Don't hesitate to come to me if you need anything.'

Eve nodded.

'Actually, this may sound a little odd but... I'm new in this city and I was wondering if you two would like to join me for dinner next week? Just so I can feel more settled and part of the team, you know?'

Amelia opened her mouth to speak before Hugh replied, 'Yes, we would love to.'

'Great.' Eve curled her lips in a close approximation of a smile. 'Wednesday at eight?'

'Sounds good, we'll see you then.' Hugh waved as Eve turned away heading in the opposite direction. Amelia glared at Hugh.

'Talk about coincidences, right Amelia?' Hugh began, completely oblivious to her expression.

'Why would you say yes for both of us? I have work to do, I don't have time to socialise.'

'Please, it's one evening, Amelia. Besides I know your schedule, you can make some time.'

'It's not just that...something seemed...off about her.' Amelia said to herself as much as she did to Hugh.

'Seemed perfectly nice to me,' Hugh replied innocently.

'Too nice.'

'You can never be too nice.'

Amelia turned back toward her desk. Her face now illuminated by the luminescent glow of her computer screen.

'Have you heard about the new AI testing their planning on the fifth floor?'

'Nope.'

'Now this could just be a rumour but...' She hesitated, unsure of whether to continue. What she was about to say could be the key to the fifth floor and she wasn't sure how many people would be let in. Though she supposed it might be nice to have Hugh with her too. He could bring her coffee.

Amelia continued, 'I heard they're working on a new line of AI, or more accurately androids, that can work amongst people. Us. Here in the office.'

'You mean like the desktop companions?'

'No. Advanced tech. Real Robosapiens if you will. You're not supposed to be able to tell the difference between us and them, but trust me, I've spent enough time around computers to know another computer when I see one.'

'Amelia, when was the last time you slept?'

Amelia stood up from her chair for emphasis.

'This is a test, Hugh, I can feel it. They're sending out these fake newbies to filter out the sceptics amongst us, the ones who don't see things the way everyone else does. The inventors! People that can pick out the flaws and help make these androids even more realistic.'

'So, you'll go with me to her house?'

'Yes. I'll go with you. To prove that that individual is a robot and that I am meant to be on the fifth floor.' Amelia smiled deviously to herself.

'Okay,' Hugh said, slightly dragging out the word, nervous to make direct eye contact. 'I'm going to get back to work.'

*

'Wow. This sure is an elaborate test,' Amelia commented, as Hugh knocked on Eve's front door. 'Whose fancy house do you think this really is? Steve from third floor? Mike from fourth?'

Truthfully, the place wasn't at all fancy. A semi-detached house painted white to match every other along the narrow London street. But compared to Amelia's tiny, cramped flat, it was like a palace.

Eve opened the door and smiled warmly. Hugh handed her a bottle of red wine that he insisted was from both of them, to which Amelia made no comment. Robots didn't drink. She invited the two inside and into her dining room where they both took a seat at a neatly prepared table, before she disappeared into the kitchen to grab some glasses.

'This is a nice place,' Hugh said, examining the Scandinavian inspired décor. Amelia, however, focused on the napkin in front of her, folded to resemble a rose bud.

'See!' Amelia held up the napkin, 'No human could fold a napkin like this.'

'It's called origami, Amelia. You really need to get out of the office more.'

Amelia sat back, slightly surprised by Hugh's sudden shift in tone. She put the napkin back and folded her arms.

*

'So how long have you too been working at Intellexia?' Eve asked as she cut into her cooked salmon.

'Wow very natural question to ask,' Amelia commented. Hugh rolled his eyes,

'I've been there two years and she's been there five.'

'I see...' replied Eve.

An awkward silence fell upon the table as the two dinner guests, struggled to again pick up the conversation. Or one. Amelia was far too busy analysing Eve's every movement to bother with trying.

'This salmon is delicious,' Hugh commented brightly. 'Cooked to perfection!'

'Yes, you're right, Hugh,' Amelia agreed. 'Do tell us does

it satisfy your taste buds? Does it appeal to your human sense of taste that you surely have, hm?'

Eve faltered. She frowned at Amelia who gave a confident smile.

'Excuse us for a moment,' said Hugh, pulling Amelia out of her seat firmly by the arm and into the corridor opposite the dining room. Hugh closed the door behind him.

'Hey, why did you drag me away, I had her at a checkmate!'

'Seriously, Amelia? By asking if she has taste buds? Look, if you're really so confident that Eve is a robot could you hurry up and prove it, because if she isn't, you're making yourself look even more suspicious with all these weird, snarky remarks.'

'Don't you worry, Hugh. I have a plan,' Amelia replied tapping the pocket of her jacket. She pulled out several folded sheets of paper and held them up to Hugh, with a devious grin. Hugh stared at them, in complete disbelief at what he was seeing, before Amelia strolled confidently back into the dining room and placed the same sheets of paper in front of Eve.

'Eve, I brought these over because I thought they'd be a fun, little team-building exercise for us all to do. You can go first. Pick out all the images with traffic lights in them.'

'Are you serious?!' Eve shouted, throwing the papers into Amelia's face.

'In her defence, she's never done well in a social setting, she's not much of a people person,' Hugh cut in. He stood defensively in front of Amelia who held on tightly to the papers, cowering behind him.

'You only came here because you thought I was some kind of android?' Eve retorted, hurt sneaking into her voice.

'You did act quite robotic,' Amelia replied quietly, but just loud enough for Eve to hear. Hugh glared at her. Eve scoffed.

'Get out of my house,' Eve stomped, emphasising each word. The two co-workers slowly backed down the hall toward the door.

'The salmon really was delicious,' Hugh began, awkwardly fumbling behind him for the door handle, 'thank you so much for—'Eve shoved the two out onto her front step in one swift motion and slammed the door in their faces.

'See you tomorrow!' Amelia called through the door. There was no response.

The two descended Eve's front steps in silence, before stopping on the pavement. For a moment neither said anything. The night was cold and dark.

'I guess she wasn't a robot,' said Amelia. Hugh smiled sadly.

'I guess not. Come on, I'll walk you back to your car,' Hugh replied, taking the lead. Amelia followed dejectedly behind him.

'I'm sorry. I don't think either of us will get invited back to hers again and I know you just wanted to hang out with some new people.'

'That's okay. I wasn't big on the salmon anyway.'

Amelia smiled. They walked in comfortable silence. As the concrete houses watched, Amelia could feel the mocking gaze of their windows.

'I'm never going to get to the fifth floor.'

'You will. You'll think of something. Maybe just forget about this whole robot conspiracy. You'll make more friends if you don't accuse them of being robots.'

Amelia chuckled. 'I guess you're right. I wouldn't accuse you of being a robot.'

'Thank you. I'll take that as a compliment,' replied Hugh.

The two reached Amelia's car. Small, but reliable.

'So, you weren't even a little bit suspicious of her?' Amelia began, pulling out her keys from her jacket pocket.

'Nope.'

'Her hair was too perfect.' Amelia opened her car door and climbed inside.

Hugh chuckled. 'Good night, Amelia. I'll see you tomorrow.'

With a gentle wave, Amelia drove away, disappearing into the darkness. Hugh waved back, smiling to himself. She really did have no idea how to recognise a real robot when she saw one, he thought.

The Owl Man

by S. P. Thane

S. P. Thane is an active poet, lyricist, vlogger, writer and podcast host.
S. P. Thane engages in many variants of writing when it comes to
storytelling through his short stories, manga/comics, poetry, music and
other amongst those.
S. P. Thane's main themes in writing blend much of real-world experience
with that of metaphorical fantasy. Attempting to gage current and new
readers with his diverse style.

Did you ever hear of The Owl Man?
WHO?
The Owl Man!
WHO?
Who is The Owl Man, to whom it may concern?

He who does not hide
He only lives in the hood of night
He walks with thoughts, wonders and ponders
On top of the trees and everything under

So, have you heard of The Owl Man?
The Who?
The Owl Man!
The Who?
No, The Owl Man, although I like their tunes
Who is the The Owl Man, to whom it may concern?

Who we may see and who he may be
The question of whom, he does not speak?
He has some teeth, but has no beak
Some have seen him, but only a peek
Is he alive if he only walks the dead of night?

So, have you heard of The Owl Man?
WHO?
The Owl Man!
WHO?
Who is The Owl Man, to whom it may concern?

They say to him the word of man lost all meaning
So, what is the point in ever speaking
A hermit, a nomad what if he is no man?
A traveller, a vagabond

A simple searcher who looks from beyond

So, who is The Owl Man?
So, you really do not know?
No! Who is the who of who you speak?
Who is the Owl Man, to me it may concern?

He is a whom's who of who to whom it may concern.

The Specific Ocean

by Corinna Keefe

Corinna Keefe is a freelance writer. She has previously published short stories and poems in Seed, Ink Sweat & Tears, Amethyst Review, and with Enthusiastic Press and Broken Sleep Books. She was a prize-winner in the Christmas Together poetry anthology from Candlestick Press.

I was strolling along Dale Road one morning when I almost tripped and fell into the sea.

It had rained the night before, and I'd stepped over several puddles already, trying to keep my battered brown shoes clean. But this was different: a faint white edge betrayed the presence of brine. A breeze ruffled the two-metre-square surface of the water and filled my lungs with cool, salt air.

There was a seagull sitting on the far edge of the sea – the puddle – looking embarrassed. It mewed half-heartedly.

'I don't suppose you can explain this, can you?' I asked. It turned its feathered back on me.

I edged closer, half-expecting the ground to fall away, or the seascape to resolve into one of those chalk pictures with odd perspective. It remained solid, but my shoes slid around in the fine white sand. A wave crashed onto the shore a few inches in front of me. I stooped to wet my fingers, and then taste, in case the seagull and the smell and the breeze had all somehow arrived through separate means.

No.

Unmistakably salt. Unmistakably sea.

I straightened up slowly and glanced around. No one was in sight, which meant that no one had witnessed me grubbing around at the edge of the sea. Puddle, I mean. It had to be a puddle.

I walked around it with my face averted and went home by a different route.

*

When I set out for my walk the next day, I decided not to go anywhere near Dale Road. And yet somehow, I found myself slowly pacing up the hill again.

Perhaps it was not such a bad thing. Once I was there, I

would see straight away that the sea had just been a puddle all along. I would feel a little silly and go home at peace.

But as I reached the crest of the hill, I realised that I was not alone. The two-metre patch of salt water was still there, and on one side, bridging the pavement and the road, was a large red-and-white striped deck chair with an old woman lying in it.

She was wearing a sensible skirt, jumper and shoes, and her hands were folded across her stomach. Her eyes were closed as if sunbathing.

I eyed her cautiously as I stooped down to check the water.

'It's still salt, you know. No change,' she said calmly.

I stepped backwards quickly.

'It doesn't make any sense,' I said.

'What doesn't?'

'This– this puddle! It shouldn't be salt!'

'And what about the seagull?'

I looked around wildly. How did she know about the seagull?

'He's under my chair,' she said. 'I always bring a few bits of bread for him, bless him. He gets a bit hungry when it's first settling in.'

'When what's settling in?'

'Why, the Ocean. When the Ocean arrives somewhere new, the fish are a bit shy for a while.'

'Why are you saying it like that?'

'Saying what like what?'

'The Ocean– like it has a capital letter. It's just a puddle! It's too small to be an ocean, or an Ocean!'

Finally, she opened her eyes and craned her neck to look directly at me.

'But it is an Ocean. And of course, it's small. Not all oceans have to be like those great big messes slopping about on the continental shelves. If it were that big, it wouldn't be the Specific Ocean.'

I gaped at her.

'You're mad,' I said at last. 'I hope someone comes and takes you home before your deckchair gets run over,' and I stomped off down the road.

'I know sarcasm when I hear it, old man!' she yelled after me.

*

On the third day, I decided not to take my walk at all. I kept myself busy and didn't even sit down for some coffee until after five o'clock, far too late for a walk.

I took my usual seat by the window overlooking the high street. I was halfway through a book, but it soon dropped to my lap while I gazed through the glass at the sun setting over the quiet town.

Except, I noticed with some annoyance, it was *not* quiet. The shops were closed, and the schools had let out long ago; but the streets seemed even busier than before. Several people were carrying towels rolled up under their arms. One man was quite definitely wielding an inflatable flamingo.

I don't know what got into me then. I flung the window open and stretched my head perilously out.

'Hey! Hey! What's happening?'

The man with the flamingo looked up and waved his pink companion cheerfully by one leg.

'We're having a beach party! Bring a few drinks if you're coming. Everyone's invited.'

'A beach party?' I said.

But he was already gone.

I resolved that I would march straight up the hill and confront the little old lady. Somehow – I could work out the details later – some way, she had filled the top of Dale Road with water and caused a public disturbance. Well, I would tell her where she could trickle off to, and her tame seagull too.

As soon as I stepped outside, I found myself in the middle of a chatting, swarming tide of people. There were young children in pushchairs, teenagers already in their swimming costumes, parents with beach bags slung over their shoulders. It was uncharacteristically warm for the time of year, with a hint of salt and smoke that caught at the back of my throat.

As I turned the corner into Dale Road, my heart sank. The shore of the Ocean was already completely obscured by beach umbrellas. Somebody was grilling sausages in the distance.

I caught a glimpse of red-and-white canvas and marched over to the old lady's deckchair. She was sitting up with the seagull on her shoulder, smiling and greeting everyone who passed.

'What on earth do you think you're doing?'

'Why, I'm enjoying an evening at the beach.'

'And what about all these other people?' I demanded.

'They're enjoying themselves too.'

'They are making a mess. They are making a noise.' I had to raise my voice to be heard. 'They are blocking a public highway!'

The old lady looked calmly up and down the street.

'I don't see any cars trying to pass through here just now, lovey. Everyone's coming for the Ocean. Why don't you go for a swim?'

'I'm not going to do that!' I raged. 'I'm not going to make *myself* ridiculous just because *you* have some ridiculous idea that you're running some kind of public service—'

'I'm not running it,' the old lady interrupted me. Her

tone had become rather steely. 'You keep talking about the Ocean like it needs planning permits and supervision and God knows what else. It's the Ocean.'

'Then who's supposed to be in charge? Who's going to supervise all these swimmers? What if—'

'Look—'

'Stop interrupting me!'

She laughed. People had started to gather round, but she remained as still in her chair as ever. She didn't seem bothered by other people at all.

'Look here. The Ocean exists. You can't do anything about it. These people are enjoying themselves. You can't really do anything about that, either. You got here too late.'

I stared at her in silence. I hated her.

'Join in,' she said, kindlier. 'You can go home, or you can join in.'

I went home.

*

I slept badly that night and woke up in the kind of mood where one drops things all the time. I smashed a coffee cup and spilt cereal on the floor.

Beach-goers! I thought, wielding the dustpan and brush with vicious concentration. People who thought that it was perfectly reasonable to circumnavigate an ocean on their way to work. Silly people. People who grilled sausages in the street. People who carried around inflatable flamingos. Fly-tippers. The kind of people whom the *neighbourhood* needed to *watch*!

The window still hung open where I had leant out the night before. There was a little wind, but it was quite different now; the air seemed stale and thin. A dirty paper plate skittered down the street. A plastic bag sagged against a lamp post.

I looked down at the shards of the cup, scattered across

the floor in a puddle of rapidly cooling coffee. I looked at the pan and brush in my hands – anaemic, dusty hands. I hadn't made time for holidays. I thought of the old lady's hands, brown and wrinkled, curled tightly in her lap. I wondered how much more rubbish must be strewn around the beach.

With a sigh, I swung my coat on over my red-and-white striped pyjamas. I stuffed a roll of black bin bags into my pocket, slipped on a pair of shoes, and set out once again for Dale Road.

The beach was almost invisible under a thick snow of paper napkins, plastic forks, deflated beach balls, mysteriously abandoned shoes, cigarette butts, soft drink bottles, and plastic cups.

'At least they were enjoying themselves,' I said aloud. With a sigh, I got to work.

I had been picking up debris for perhaps half an hour when I lifted a napkin and saw the lady smiling up at me. She had been quite buried.

'Good morning,' she said.

'Good morning,' I said, shortly. Then: 'I'm sorry.'

'I'm glad you're here,' she replied. 'I hoped you would come back.'

'I didn't want you to be left up here on your own,' I said, feeling rather foolish. 'I mean I– I didn't think it was fair that you should have to clean up on your own.'

'Well, I think I might walk into town and get us a cup of tea. Do you mind finishing up?'

'Not at all,' I said. I brushed a few more scraps of rubbish aside as she levered herself stiffly up out of the deckchair.

'I'll be back soon,' she said.

'No rush,' I said.

*

After 45 minutes, there were six fat black rubbish bags sitting by the side of the road. The beach remained quiet, even though it was a baking hot day. I'd discarded my coat long ago. There was still no sign of the old lady.

I undid the buttons of my pyjama shirt and hung it carefully over the deckchair. I rolled my pyjama trousers tightly up to the knee and kicked off my shoes.

The first touch of the waves against my toes was like the first sip of water after a long, desperate night. I felt the ripples spread out calmly across my mind. I shuffled forward, sighing as the sand caressed my feet, pieces of shell and sea-glass turning up to glint in the morning light. There was a bubbling white edge of foam to the waves which bounced up at me in greeting. The sun scattered off the water in a thousand tiny dawns.

I walked out until the water was chest-deep and dove into the arms of the Ocean. It was cool, so deliciously cool after working in the heat and muck. Tiny currents clasped my hands. Salt water flowed over my face and I opened my eyes. It was quite clear.

My feet groped for the Ocean floor and found smooth rock. Little fish flocked around my ankles. Above me, light flickered through the greenish water, and sunbeams reached down like the columns of some vast hall. I swam in and out of them, marvelling.

The Specific Ocean stretched around me, above me, in fathomless depths and distances which had been invisible from the surface. It was a whole world – a whole specific world – vast, tiny, and everywhere unmistakably itself.

When at last I came to the surface, I kicked up my legs and lay on my back, arms spread wide. The waves moved gently against my side, and I turned diagonally to the tide so that I could lie still. I heard the seagull cry in the distance.

After a long time, someone called out:

'Hello!'

I paddled myself upright and looked toward the shore, shading my eyes with one hand. It was the lady, clutching a small brown paper bag.

'Hello! I've brought you tea! And a Chelsea bun!'

'I'll come right out!' I shouted back and began to swim. I pulled and kicked in a steady breaststroke, feeling stronger than I had in years. Salt water was meant to be good for the health, I remembered.

'Did you have a good swim?' said the old lady.

'I certainly did, thanks,' I said. 'And thanks for the tea.'

'It's just the thing after being in the water,' she said. 'Myself, I like to swim first thing in the morning. It gets cold in winter, but they say it keeps you young. And a hot flask of tea will set you up for the day afterwards.'

I sat on the sand beside her deckchair while we ate in companionable silence. I amused myself by throwing crumbs of Chelsea bun for the seagull to fetch.

'May I ask you something?' I said, eventually.

'Of course.'

'How— How long does the Ocean usually stay? In one place, I mean?'

She leant back in her deckchair and stared thoughtfully at the sky.

'Depends where the Ocean feels at home, feels welcome. It usually likes to move on after a storm. Storms shake things up, like.'

'Did you come here after a storm?'

'After many storms,' she said, and laughed to herself.

'Do you get tired of it?'

'Of the Ocean? No. But I do get tired of moving, sometimes.'

'Do you think you'll ever stop?'

'This has been a lot more than one question.'

I nodded. Stretched. Stood up.

'I think it's time I ought to be moving off myself.'

'Will you come again tomorrow?' she said. She looked worried, suddenly.

'I'm not sure. I'll see how things go.'

'All right,' she said. Her cramped hands twisted nervously in her lap. 'Be seeing you, then.'

I hesitated.

'Look, I don't know about tomorrow. But if you should need anything – I live down on New Street. Number 84 . There's a spare key under the doormat.'

She looked up at me with relief.

'Thank you.'

'Be seeing you,' I said hastily, and left.

There was a strange wind at my back as I walked down Dale Road. By the time I reached the house, thick black clouds were gathering. I shivered in my damp pyjamas and made sure the shutters were closed before I went to bed.

*

The storm raged for two days and two nights. Those same black clouds unleashed the heaviest rain in years and gale-force winds ripped around the corners of the streets. Warnings came in over the radio and television, telling everyone to stay indoors and get animals under shelter.

I stayed in my sitting room, in an agony of worry about the lady and the Ocean. She would be quite exposed up there on the hill. Worst of all, she had said that the Specific Ocean often moved on after a storm. By the time it was safe to go outside, the Ocean might have disappeared altogether. I knew I would never find it again.

Early on the third day, I was woken by an unfamiliar silence. The rain had stopped and the wind had gone down. Everything was quiet. I lay back for a second, relishing the peace; then I thought of the Ocean.

I flew out of bed and pulled on my clothes. I made a flask of hot tea in the biggest Thermos I could find. I looked in the biscuit tin and found a few stale ones left – those would do for the seagull.

I checked over the house thoroughly before I left. By some miracle no tiles had come off and all the shutters stood firm. I closed the door behind me with a snap.

Some instinct made me check under the doormat. The spare key was still there, despite the storm. Just in case somebody should need it.

I set off up the hill at a run, the Thermos and biscuit tin banging around in my rucksack.

The Ocean was still there. It was. The waters seemed grey and muddier than before, with hanks of seaweed tossed up on to the surface, but they were still indisputably Ocean, just as they had been on that first day when I was so furiously reluctant to believe.

The sand was whipped up into dunes and wild shapes by the wind and driftwood lay scattered along the shore. The deckchair was lying near the waterline, overturned on its side.

I approached it nervously, but it was empty. I felt enormously relieved, and for a second didn't know why, until the thought came into my mind: no body. Wherever the lady was, she was not here. She had found somewhere else to be.

I felt something pecking hopefully at my feet. It was the seagull. I turned the deckchair right-side up and sat down in it gently. Slowly, trying not to startle the bird, I took out the biscuit tin. I sprinkled a few crumbs on the sand at my feet.

'There you go, Mr Gull,' I said. I put my feet up and settled back into the chair.

I must have dozed off for a few minutes.

*

After so many days of rain and thunder, the sun felt
unusually warm on my face. Hardly English at all. I opened
my eyes and stretched luxuriously.

There the Ocean was, still breaking and chattering
quietly by my side. The seagull had hopped up beside me
and was busily clanging around in the biscuit tin. In the
distance, I caught a glimmer of pink.

Over on the far side of the Specific Ocean, a flamingo was
standing on one leg, peacefully snoozing.

Sunday on the Boulevard (with my Pet Lobster)

by Dale Hurst

Dale Hurst is an English novelist, poet, journalist, and broadcaster. As a writer, he specialises in historical and mystery fiction.
Having dabbled in writing in various formats since he was ten, he published his first novel, the mystery The Berylford Scandals: Lust & Liberty in 2018. A sequel, Sin & Secrecy, followed in 2020.
Dale is also the presenter of The Dale Hurst Writing Show, a podcast discussing issues surrounding writing, publishing, and storytelling.

I'd like to introduce you to a unique pet of mine. A creature with whom I shared many a happy moment. You may think I've gone round the twist when I tell you that I found my life's companion in the form of a lobster.

Cats are aloof and always seem to be scheming, while dogs have their boisterous habits. I don't even care to recall the trouble we had cleaning up after our budgerigar. But keeping a lobster required no lifestyle changes or excess of affection. In fact, mine demonstrated a mutual love of the finer things in life. In particular...a penchant for Montecristo cigars.

Now don't ask me how a lobster smokes – they are not especially loquacious creatures. All I can say is that after his meal of shrimp bisque (not cannibalism, before you ask), he would clamber out of his tank, grab a Montecristo from the case, snip off the end with a claw you'd think was made for the job, and, once I had lighted it for him, would smoke it. You don't get such refinement and elegance with a tabby, a Labrador, or your standard tropical aquarium fish!

Of course, taking him out in public turned a few heads. With twice as many smokers in the house now, we were going through the Montecristos in half the time. And Monsieur le Verrier, our local tobacconist, was almost appalled to find a crustacean in his shop.

"Monsieur François!" I remember he cried. "*Qu'est-ce que c'est?* A lobster on your shoulder!"

"You were expecting a parrot? A giant squid? A girl from the Folies Bergère? Or perhaps even Humphrey Bogart himself?"

Poor Monsieur le Verrier – too often have I seen his face scrunch up like a bewildered little prune with a shoe brush under its nose to serve as a moustache. Ever since I have been a customer at his very accommodating, if shabby, little shop, I have always held the opinion that he is a man quite pitiful. A dilapidated mole of a man who seems so exhausted by life that he remains deliberately ignorant of all around him for the sake of some peace. It's difficult not to take the tiniest sadistic pleasure in his inability to tell whether I'm being serious or not.

"You are in here sooner than usual, Monsieur," he declared, still frowning almost fearfully at the bluish-black shellfish clicking its claws atop my coat, "We did not expect you for another fortnight."

"Another mouth to feed, you see, Monsieur le Verrier, so I will require a double-order of Montecristos this time s'il vous plaît."

Monsieur le Verrier looked close to bursting into tears when he gleaned that I was talking about my pet lobster.

"But, Monsieur—" he began, "The lobster? Surely it can't—"

"And why on earth not?"

I placed my money on his counter to demonstrate how insistent I was.

"Very well," the befuddled little tobacconist gave in, "*Vingt-huit de la Montecristo. Cinquante francs, s'il vous plaît.*"

I gave him seventy, a tip for his trouble. After all, how many tobacconists go through their lives selling cigars to lobsters? They surely don't learn that in the training! My lobster snapped his claws again, I assumed with great joy and readiness to break in his new box of Montecristos.

"Monsieur François, a moment more of your time," Monsieur le Verrier beckoned me closer, "I have just recalled a piece of information my brother told me once about keeping lobsters."

"Ah yes, of course – Monsieur *Jacques* le Verrier from the zoo!" I recollected the man in question – an eminent and esteemed expert in his field – at once, "Well what is this advice?"

"That lobsters are prone to coughing. But if you feed it an asparagus, it should go away."

"What excellent advice!" I revelled with glee. "There will be plenty of coughing to come if he likes these cigars so much!"

"Plenty of asparagus too, in that case," Monsieur le Verrier was still looking most unsure about the lobster on my shoulder, "He may not like it at first, but just shove it in and, sooner or later, he will take it. Like you're stuffing a duck for foie gras."

"You are most kind, Monsieur!" I said, "And you must pass on my regards to your brother!"

"Oh, I would, but I cannot."

"Why ever not?"

"He slipped and fell into the shark tank at the zoo, with a bleeding toe. It was a feeding frenzy within seconds."

"*Mon Dieu!*" I gasped, "Quelle dommage! The secret is sticking with smaller creatures – they present far fewer dangers!"

The lobster snipped at my earlobe with his claw – evidently getting impatient. Just chomping at the bit for a Montecristo.

"Well, merci beaucoup, Monsieur le Verrier," I hastily conceded, "I'll be back in two weeks."

*

It was such a glorious Sunday, I decided to take my companion out to dinner at *Chez l'Armoire* right off the Boulevard Sainte Lourdes de Biarritz. The incomparable views of the glistening, crystal sea can only be got from an al fresco seat on the veranda of this top-class restaurant. But like poor Monsieur le Verrier, I fear the hostess did not quite understand my pet. She looked absolutely horrified when she came to take our order and, to my dismay, went to confiscate my lobster.

"*Excusez-moi!*" I protested, "What do you think you are doing? This is a pet-friendly restaurant!"

"But Monsieur!" replied the hostess, "The lobster – she is not cooked!"

"*He* is here to eat!"

"Pardon?" the hostess' voice reduced almost to a whimper; she was so confused.

"This is dinner for *two*, mademoiselle! And the lobster will have shrimp bisque to start, with an asparagus salad to follow."

At the mention of asparagus, the lobster began to splutter, which quite frankly scared the hostess out of her skin. I could not blame her in actual fact. The sound of a lobster coughing is quite extraordinary – not the sort of thing one could predict. Like a cat trying to hack up a hairball while having its head stuffed rather unceremoniously into a paper bag at the same time. A crackly and snappy kind of retching.

"On second thought," I piped up. "Bring the asparagus first, and the bisque for afters. And perhaps a little caviar? Wait a minute – do you want the cocktail menu, or shall we share a bottle of champagne?" I directed the question to the lobster, who quite frankly did not look too fussed one way or the other – as long as the much-needed asparagus arrived first.

"All right! All right! The champagne then! A bottle of the Pierre Beauvais, s'il vous plaît," I silkily requested from the hostess.

Off she went, shaking her head every few steps as though this was the oddest thing she had ever seen. In her line of work, surely not! All sorts of people and pets must come through the doors of *Chez l'Armoire*! I heard of the Comtesse de Montreuil bringing her pelican for a lunch with her friends, and the actress Ingrid Oberfeldt made the headlines by holding a birthday party for the family's beloved tarantula. My lobster – his unprecedented predilection for smoking notwithstanding – was surely quite mundane by comparison.

The asparagus salad was brought soon after and placed down in front of the lobster. The hostess did not linger to observe, which in truth was probably for the best. It made for rather chaotic work, trying to feed a lobster a stalked vegetable. Its mouth did not seem big enough to eat it, but Monsieur le Verrier's advice rang in my head: 'Just shove it in and, sooner or later, he will take it.'

And eventually, he did. But the added exercise of consuming the thing made us both in the mood for a cigar, which we indulged in as our main courses came out – my duck roasted with olives and caviar, and the lobster's sumptuous bisque.

There was no time for dessert, for after his dinner, the lobster began to cough again. So, smuggling out the remaining asparagus, I took him for some fresh air along the boulevard, turning the heads of many a passerby as we did so. The lobster hardly seemed interested in the asparagus, for all his spluttering. He seemed as tempted as I to just dive into that flawless sea water. But I was hardly dressed for the occasion, and he could not possibly go in coughing all over the place. Once more, I stuffed a green stalk down him.

The coughing did stop eventually, but I came to suspect it was not the asparagus that did the trick. Because my lobster died while on the Boulevard Sainte Lourdes de Biarritz. The story you have just heard is the same one I told Monsieur le Verrier the following day, when I went to confront him rather indignantly about his late brother's ultimately dubious advice.

"You told me that the coughing would go away if I force-fed the lobster asparagus!" I quite rightly told him, "What do you have to say for yourself?"

"Well, Monsieur, you may have done that part, but you missed one rather vital step in looking after a lobster!"

"Do you think it was the cigars that killed him?" I asked.

"I highly doubt they helped matters, but there's something even more basic that he should have had."

"What's that?"

"Well, he was a lobster, Monsieur. You should have kept him in some water!"

Consequences

by Shannon Savvas

A New Zealand writer who divides her life between New Zealand, England, and Cyprus.
Shortlisted for The Bridport Prize, Kilmore Literary Festival Write by the Sea, Allingham Festival in 2021. Longlisted for Sligo Cairde Short Story Award, Flash500. Was nominated for the 2020 Pushcart. Won a few, lost more. Made a few shortlists, longlists, and published online, in anthologies and magazines.

By late summer, the days slow and the nights swelter.
The air, thick with pine-scented resin, myrtle and thyme,
induces languor in both mortals and immortals. It drives
Hermes mad, because for him it is not business as usual. It
is not business at all.

In the busy seasons, guiding dead souls and delivering
the Gods' missives is 24/7 and Hermes has been known to
mix the two up. Like the time he confused the golden bow
and arrows wrapped in pale silks from Lord Ares to Lady
Artemis with the dead senator wrapped in pale linens for
dispatch to the Underworld. Uncle Hades was delighted
with his new toys, but the tantrum Lady Artemis threw
after she unwrapped a corpse instead of the weaponry
she'd ordered, meant Hermes had to wear his helmet of
invisibility for a month.

But this time of the year, messenger business is slow and
fewer souls need a guide to the Underworld.

On the golden plains, mortals cling to life, loathe to risk
life or limb or to expend energy beyond the necessary; to
eat, to fuck, to bathe, to...to...well, there isn't much else.

Preferring the shade of their villas to the shadows of
Erebus, the aristocracy hide from the onslaught of sun.
They sleep late in their privilege, idling away the days
protected by cool stone and deep inner pools, waited on by
houseboys and slaves. By night, serviced by concubines, of
all persuasions, the elite drink the last of the year's wines
and gorge on the benevolence of the season's abundance.

But in these burning, brutal months, nobody, not even
the hoi polloi, worked hard. The prevailing exhaustion
was not the malignant sort, but the kind that came from
nights rousing in inns or rutting in brothels tended and
pimped by porn-shepherds, who sold their *obols* of flesh
and who never, ever went out into the light of day. It was
the exhaustion of indolence. Some called it a little gift of

the gods, this time when nobody divine or mortal could be arsed.

The Gods don't meddle during summer, preferring a bit of R&R in their cool mountains and leafy woodland retreats. Hermes, a child at heart who needs constant distraction and is restless in his boredom, jumps when Dad sends a white raven to summon him. He slaps on his wingèd sandals and helmet, grabs his satchel and caduceus, leaving his tortoise and rooster to their stir-crazy madness, to fly to Zeus's latest super-deluxe, razzamatazz sanctuary on Mount Olympus. Mount Olympus where Hephaestus has built the Gods their Very Serious Convening Palace. Because of his inferiority complex and doomed to ungodly imperfection by a very gammy leg, Hephaestus had gone way OTT and out the other side to curry favour and avoid offence. Piling on the sycophancy, he plastered the palace with gilded depictions of their attributes, feats, and frankly bullshit beauty.

Following the raven's slipstream between the colonnades, Hermes balks his first landing at the sight of all twelve flashing, dashing, cue inverted commas, GODS. Elevated by three flights of white granite steps, surrounded by pink and black-veined marble columns, they loom, swollen with self-importance on their thrones. He circles around for a second approach but as he comes in to land, perspiration, brought on by the speed of the flight and trepidation at the sight of the assembly, stings his eyes. He fluffs touchdown completely, stumbles, stubs his toe, tumbles forward and pulls up just short of smashing into the lower step of the sacred Stairway to the Heavens.

Twelve pairs of delusional eyes watch Hermes right himself. He straightens his helmet. The wing on his left sandal flaps like a broken shutter.

Bugger, that'll cause problems.

Shamed by the tittering and sniggering, he fumbles with it.

'Such a smooth operator.'

Hera!

Like all of Zeus's offspring not born of her self-appointed golden loins, Hermes suffers from his stepmother's spite. He is wary.

Aphrodite scampers down, hands him his staff with a sweet smile and a twinkle in her eyes.

She may be a tart, but she's a nice tart... Hermes is grateful.

Hermes takes a quick shifty round. Po-faced Athena, always the superior moody cow, still preening from her recent besting of Poseidon, lets her smirk do the talking. That smirk, which will endure for millennia until it simply becomes known as wearing a Patel. Silence is how she got her reputation for wisdom; keep schtum and everyone thinks you're clever. But Hermes knows better.

Next to Athena, Artemis scowls, her pretty, top lip curled in an unvoiced snarl. She was clearly still pissed about the dead senator.

Who cares? She dares not touch me here. Not in front of Dad.

'Whenever you are ready, Hermes.' Zeus is impatient.

Cripes, this is big.

'Yes Sir, ready.'

'Find that lout, Dionysus. Tell him we want him here, immediately.'

Hermes doesn't need telling twice. He begins his lift off.

'I haven't finished.'

Hermes drops like a stone. 'Sorry, Dad.'

Zeus's glare is Gorgons-grade.

Bugger. Not Dad. Not Dad. Not Dad. Dad is a stickler for protocol.

'Sorry, Sir.'

'We also want his gang of reprobates. Hypnos, Eros, Priapus and Morpheus, make sure that one leaves his poppies behind.' Zeus looks at his fellow Olympians. 'What do they call themselves?'

'The Liberators,' says Ares resplendent in his gleaming armour. 'As if.'

'One more thing, Hermes,' Zeus says, narrowing his eyes.

Oh hell, he's heard about the party on Rhodes.

'No exceptions, no excuses, understood?'

'Understood, Sir.'

'What are you waiting for, boy? Applause?'

'N-no Sir. Yes Sir. Sorry Sir. Right. You've finished? Right, I'm off.' Hermes rises but at speeding-off altitude, he flies in tight right-hand circles, like a demented bee in front of the whole supercilious congregation. The bloody broken wing has knocked his steering alignment out.

It takes an hour to fix, but once done, he's away. Hermes is pump, pump, pumped. An urgent directive from Olympus itself. Head Honcho. Big Daddy. Zeus himself.

He knows where to find Dio. Every year, as the new grapes grow heavy and lush, Dionysus's personal mission is to finish last year's wine before the new harvest. The guy parties methodically north to south. Hermes punches a couple of bumbling pigeons out of his way as he turns south, such is his delight.

At Oinopolis, Hermes finds Dio snoring under a barrel, his mouth positioned to catch the dribs and drabs from the uncorked funnel. Dio's golden diadem of vine leaves is buried in the dust beside him, his tunic sodden with regurgitated wine, his breath rancid.

Hermes toes Dio. Nothing.

'Come on, wake up.' He prods Dio's gelatinous belly with his staff until one of Dio's eyelids unstick a bleary fraction before squeezing shut again.

'Dio! Dio, come on.'

'Hermes, you piece of goat's crap, Hephaestus' anvil is hammering in my head, and unless you have a very, and I mean very, good reason to be here, I'm going to shove you head first through the plughole of this cask. Three guesses where the bloody cork will go.' His words scritch and squeeze out of his dry lips.

'Zeus wants to see you, like yesterday.'

Dionysus bolts upright and clutches his head.

'Oh shit. Oh shit, my head. Oh shit. What have I done? What does he want? Oh shit.'

'Dunno. But they want you, Morpheus, Hypnos and Eros as well. And what's his name with the big dick...Priapus?'

Dionysus's eyes, cherry blossom pink without the charm, blink. His tongue, a terminal shade of icterus, swabs his bulbous lips. 'What do you mean *they*?'

'The Twelve.' Hermes twirls Dio's diadem on his foot.

'*All* Twelve? What the hell...give me that, sonny?' Dio grabs his crown and slips it on his head.

'Dio, if I were you...'

'Well, you're not are you, you jumped up carrier pigeon?' Dionysus looks as brittle as he sounds.

Hermes drifts upwards. 'At least I can see straight. Like I say, unless you are tired of being you, you know how vindictive Dad is, I'd have a bath, round up your mates and get over to Olympus PDQ. I'm off, but make sure you're sober before you arrive,' he shouts, disappearing into the glare of the sun beating down on Dionysus cradling his head.

*

Thirty-six hours it takes. Thirty-six hours calling in and promising favours to locate the boys recovering in their bolt-holes after the summer of parties, booze and sex. Best bender ever, Eros had called it some weeks back. At his age, he wasn't ready to stop partying and left the oldies to wind down. Dio left for one last quiet crack at Oinopolis. Morpheus, after a summer fuelled by his beloved poppies, was time-travelling with goats. Only when his brother, Phobetor, put the fear of the Titans and Ephialtes into him, did he emerge from his drugged stupor. Their Father, Hypnos, an impotent debauchee in his dotage, had tried schmoozing up to his wife Nyx, the Goddess of Night, for a bit of slap-and-tickle a week ago. She was pissed as hell, and not in a happy way. She had drawn him into a deep sleep which he couldn't shake off. As a result, he stumbled, farted and tried to curl up asleep every time he stopped moving. As for Eros, after a love fest with a very pretty band of boys in Ephesus, he could barely walk.

'You'd think his anus never had any wrinkles,' says Priapus, who while exhausted, is undefeated from his own extended orgy.

Thirty-six hours is too long and not enough to get the gang presentable. Sober would take longer and they don't have that much time. Dread urges them into some semblance of order. Dishevelled and hungover, they pitch up at Olympus, wilting under the chorus mask stares of the Twelve who are once more seated on thrones in the shaded portico of the Royal Hall. Only Aphrodite smiles when she spies her son Eros.

'Looks like Medusa's given them the once over,' Dionysus burps *sotto voce* to a still-stoned Morpheus.

Hypnos taking advantage of Priapus's abundant member leans against it, trying to stay upright, fighting to keep his eyes open.

The Gods, tight-lipped and silent, wait for Zeus to begin while the Gang of Five sweat and shuffle in the hot open courtyard at the base of the steps.

'Good of you to join us,' Zeus says.

Like we had a choice.

Worried by the sarcasm in His Lordship's voice, Dionysus keeps the snipe behind his teeth, deep in his throat.

Eros, his eyes watering, carefully lowers one cheek to perch on the lower step.

'Who said you could sit?' roars out of Zeus. Eros yelps, scurrying upright. 'And what, by the Heavens, took you so long?'

'Well, Zeus, baby, it wasn't easy, you know,' Morpheus giggles. 'We, uh, we...'

'Shut up, shut up, shut up,' Dionysus hisses.

'Speak when you're spoken to, is that clear?' Zeus says. 'You've been summoned for a serious matter, so listen very carefully.'

In the dutiful silence, Hypnos lets rip a twenty-second fart. Definitely virtuoso. Definitely the opening notes of Pan's much-loved tune, *Glory to the Elysian Heroes*. Shock and awe ripple the silence.

Zeus leans forward on his throne, presses his knuckles against his clenched mouth and looks to his brother, Poseidon.

Poseidon, tired of playing second fiddle to his brother, still humiliated by the city's preference for Athena and her lousy olives, wastes no time. Striding forward, trident in hand poised and ready to smote should the chance arise, this is his moment. He swells with righteousness.

'It is the considered opinion of us all,' he intones with gravity, 'that the state of affairs produced by the combined effects of your unlicensed drunkenness, lechery, laziness, excess, disrespect, poppy pushing, debauchery, carnal...'

'Get on with it.' Zeus closes his eyes with patent exasperation.

'Yes, well you get the picture,' Poseidon says, deliberately blocking Athena's frenzied head-bobbing, first from one side, then the other in her eagerness to be seen.

'My Lord Zeus, this is ridiculous,' Athena says. 'As the Peoples' Choice, surely I—'

'Quiet. My brother speaks.'

'Thank you, Brother. As always, true wisdom.' Poseidon hides a smirk from Zeus but not Athena before turning back to Dionysus and his motley crew. 'The mortals are being led astray by your antics and temptations. They are neglecting homes, work and families. And what is worse and far more important is they are not paying any attention to us. Something needs to be done.' Not being privy to what needs to be done, he finishes with a piercing look at each of the five and sits down.

The reprobates look at each other. Hypnos twigs this is serious but seriously considers whether he really gives a shit. Priapus sags ever so slightly until he is left with a half-mongrel under his cloak. Dionysus and Morpheus are suddenly stone-cold sober. Only Eros, too busy making googly eyes at Narcissus waiting his turn for an audience with the Gods to request a proper mirror instead of the rippling river to look at himself, remains oblivious.

As team leader, Dionysus knows he must respond. Gagging for a drink, even water would be welcome, he licks his parched lips.

'But my Lords and Ladies.' He smiles obsequiously as his mind races seeking wriggle room. 'These very...ah...these very talents, attributes, if you will, were bestowed on us by you. What would you have us do?' He ends with a deep bow and a wide flourish of his arm.

'What's the bow in aid of, idiot?' whispers Morpheus.

Dionysus shrugs. 'It seemed a good idea. Hell, have you any better ideas?'

Zeus stands on the uppermost step and looks down at them.

'You don't need to do anything. Rightly, as you point out, you have been given these...whatever. Once given there's no taking back. So, they need a counter balance.'

The other gods start muttering and nodding behind him.

'Hear, hear.'

'About time.'

'Absolutely.'

'Finally.'

Zeus holds up his hand for silence.

No farts this time.

The five purse their lips, furrow their brows and shoot each other questioning looks. Sobriety returns, sleep departs and lust goes walkabout. Whatever is coming is coming now and they aren't looking forward to it.

Zeus claps his hands.

To everyone's surprise, in walk seven stunning maidens and, to Eros's delight, three handsome strapping lads.

'These are your new assistants. They will introduce themselves. I have given them names which sound odd but trust me, they will take them to eternity and back.' He nods to the newcomers. 'Go ahead.'

One by one, each steps forward to announce his or herself. Some of the terms are gobbledygook but will carry down the ages because the gods are omnipotent and foresee the rise of the barbaric Romans.

'Syphilis.'

'Gonorrhea.'

'Chlamydia.'

'Cachexia.'

'Nausea.'

'Vertigo.'

'Insomnia.'

'Verruca.'
'Hepatitis.'
'Delirium.'

Acrylic Eyes Yellowing Under Strip Lights in Acton

By Ben Verinder

Ben Verinder lives in rural Hertfordshire. His first pamphlet was published by Frosted Fire, the publishing arm of the Cheltenham Poetry Festival, in autumn 2021. Ben is an amateur mycologist, a wild food forager and the biographer of the adventurer and writer Mary Burkett. He is currently studying a Writing Poetry MA with Newcastle University.

"Contrary to myth, Tussauds waxworks are never melted down to make new ones. They just go into storage." *Daily Mirror*, 21 October 2011

They came to mob whatever extract gave us power
scratch a nub of us beneath their fingernails,
frot us in the darker corridors then splurge
our currency down the Marylebone Road
but now we are stocked in rows.
Don't get blood on my shirt! Kennedy jokes
as Cobain fondles a cartridge between fingertips
smooth as soap. In winter, our hair rots
but this heat oozes us out of lousy clothes
as we watch Rutherford on her knees hunting eyebrows.
Gorbachev's port stain dribbles to his ear
and Victoria's fat head sinks into black bombazine
like the sun going down on Empire.
No visitor in weeks, only traffic rumbling
its imitation of the touch-up artist's trolley
and, from the workshop, a sewing hive,
voices, the gulp of boiling wax
poured into moulds. A revolution
is a struggle between futures and the past,
Castro replays. Voltaire is tongueless;
Ali, pinned by masonry bolts and webbing.
Frank won't leave the breeze of her open window.
Newman lost a hand. Even the Bonds are breaking.

Echo Land

by Celeste Engel

*Celeste Engel completed a Masters in Writing for the Media at
Bournemouth University in 2011. Celeste has had three short films
produced. She has directed six multi-media plays; was shortlisted for
the Kenneth Branagh Writing Prize in 2015 for her play SHINE BRIGHT
her play SWEET DREAMS received a development package from Theatre
West in 2021. Since 2012 Celeste has been working at the Arts University
Bournemouth on the Filmmaking Short Course.*

Like the prodigal
I returned
Arrived back to place and people
Vibrant in my colouring
To discover I had become,

A ghost
A whisper
A haunting as I haunted
An echo of moments past
A dream one struggles to remember
I no longer knew where I was
Navigated my way like a bat
Using past echoes to feel my way through worlds

I travelled time
My lungs led me to Air
Tumbled me away like a weed
I found myself dancing on new winds

A tornado tidal with expectation

The voices, the faces, the violence of your places
You storied me to sleep
The missing, an ache
A whole perforated by absence
I empty lying foetal in new world humming
I gaze back, tie myself to you tight
Lie in sleep, yet walk days unnumbered
Scream through one way mirror, invisible
I the dream, the echo
A whisper, indecipherable
The dappled light of sparkled diamond memory
Whose tales have you returning to memorised phrase

Morning light brings a clarity that exiles the fog

I sang your waves in and called your waves out
Paused your tidal pull on a whim
Made your waves crash with an arm swish boom

That was when, I was home…home was you
Home was then, I will never be at home again
I am a prism made up of mirrored shards

Reflecting light whilst straining against the glass

I am the dew evaporated by morning sun
Loss tints my gaze and colours all I see

A cacophony of hues make up my symphony
I am a ghost in a country full of spectres

Somebody's Home

by Naomi McClaughry

Naomi was born in Northern Ireland and grew up on a farm by the Irish border. Born after the Good Friday Agreement, she strives to write honest pieces on the, frequently, misrepresented communities of this part of the world. She is also a keen performance poet, using her own dialect with pride. She is currently studying Creative Writing as an undergraduate at Arts University Bournemouth.

It started when I found myself sleeping for far too long
each night. The kind of sleep that leaves you waking up
even more tired than the night before. Now, I'm cornering
strangers in the shop for excessively long spats of small talk
and making extended eye contact with people on the bus. I
have checked my symptoms online, tried to figure out what
sort of illness I am cursed with but to no avail. There is no
medical diagnosis for this predicament.

It's been years since I practiced but it's the type of skill
that never weakens, it's instinctive once you know the
tricks. My boots tightly laced in front of the fireplace are
raring to go.

The fire is blazing as I throw
    tea leaves to the flames.
      An old cork
        between my fingertips,
          it's tossed too.
           A splash of perfume
            makes the colours flash
            and just as they soften,
          I drip in
            the wax of a candle

"'When this smoke takes flight, when it reaches the end
of the deep sky, dissipating into clouds, my movement is
finally nigh.'" I pause for a second, breathe in the remnants
of the evaporated perfume and stand.

Marching out into the cold air, I smell smoke as it grits
against my nose filling me with carbon that my body
hates. I don't mind because it smells good. It smells like
somebody is home. I place my shoes in the muddy grass
and trek up the steep incline. It takes five minutes, but
it feels like a never-ending journey, unsure of where the
highest point really is. I am simply guessing day by day

Atop the hill, I can see swirls of smoke taking the escalator to heaven from every ancient farmhouse within a half mile radius, or however far my eyes can see. The smoke is taking an escape route from the cramped rooms and dry air, spiralling out into the atmosphere. I spot the smog of my fire as it twinkles against the mid-morning light. I do not linger but focus in on a cottage five fields and a narrow road away. The smoke from that chimney dances like a troupe of baby ballerinas, cluttered and all over the place but still a beautiful, fluffy flurry.

One step, two step
and twirl.

'Beautiful, beautiful!'

Pas de deux,
I am part of the performance.

One step, two step -
I twirl.
This is adagio,
gentle and soft.

The smoke rises above me as the performance reaches its finale.

My tutu spins out, the smoke spreading in the wind as I gently float down the chimney, landing in a perfect plié.

The knees I have adopted don't take the landing well as they jolt back into place with a painful ache. This body is stiff, I feel the weight of a lifetime on their back. The room we're in is obnoxiously warm and the walls a curious yellow, like a sepia-toned filter or a weathered photograph. I feel a nudge on their leg and look down to see a sheep dog, black and white. As they stroke its fur, I notice the hand is much larger and more wrinkled than mine. I keep petting and eventually check the tag on its collar,

'We'll get the tea boiling yet, Shep.' The speech comes out without warning, as if it skipped the inner monologue stage. They navigate through the household to the kitchen, but I stop us at a mirror in the hallway. This man's hair is thick and white, like purified smoke. I go to smile but instead a sigh is heard and the journey to the kettle continues, Shep leaving muddy pawprints behind us.

The counters are overflowing with still sealed packets of biscuits, as the fridge is opened, I see countless premade meals, some already mouldy. A recently vacated wake house. After the kettle is full and in motion, I begin to wander the room, I pick up a stray funeral order, Mary Black 1937-2021. I feel a trickle run down our cheek. The kettle flicks and he immediately drops the thin booklet. His hand shakes as he adds one, two, three, four sugars to the tea, then pours in a frightening amount of milk. We shuffle back to the fireplace.

He directs our eyesight to a chair opposite his own and hovers. I attempt to turn the gaze or even lift his tea, but he stares with strong intention. Eventually a pipe is pulled out and as he tamps down the tobacco, Shep nudges in close, as if he too is addicted. The smoke starts rising and I feel myself travel out of his body and up through the pipe. Staining the wallpaper on our way out.

> The thickest smoke,
>> matted sheep's wool,
> is the heaviest.
> Tar,
>> tobacco
> and too many
>> regrettable moments.
Grime that should
>> stay

>> down

on earth.
You'd think it   too heavy to rise
but the science,   cold and warm air,
prevails.
So, I   f l o a t   until I find fresh smoke.

'Out with the old and in with the new.' I'm in front of a
bonfire. Furniture and old paperwork is piled up beginning
to disintegrate. These knees don't ache, but the shoulders
are tense. The head turns to our right and a smile is
directed at the person who just spoke, a woman who must
be in her early 30s. They glance at the fire again and I sense
our stomach tightening.

'I feel a little bad – these were someone's lifelong
possessions.' This voice is feminine and sounds just as
young as her – eye contact – her partner.

'Yes, lifelong. Not alive now, are they?' I feel our lips
curling up in an almost laugh but just before the sound
comes out,

'You're horrible. Let's unpack more.' We follow the
woman indoors and start unboxing minimal kitchen ware.
The cupboards are old and worn, the tiles a dated green,
not like the trendy forest shade that every millennial seems
to love.

'I cannot wait to get in here done up.' I feel a tug in her
chest pushing us to disagree, but we don't, instead she
starts wiping down the cupboards. The other woman exits
the room to check on the fire causing the cloth wiping the
counter to move faster and faster. As the motion becomes
wearing, I take my chance and bring it to a halt. Her
breathing is heavy, and the lungs feel strained, pushing
clumps of emotion out alongside carbon dioxide. She grips
the counter and I force her breaths to slow, taking time to
fully swallow as much oxygen as possible.

When her lungs have found peace again, she glances

around the room, wandering over to a box of framed photographs. The largest is a wedding picture, the two of them in casual clothing in front of a shabby town hall. A lightness enters her body, like a rush of wind, and I can just about see the reflection of a smile in the frame's glass.

Her wife re-enters the room with a money plant covered in Christmas lights and tiny ornaments.

'I didn't want to wait to get a proper tree.' A quick succession of tingles through the chest, then we're hugging, and it's settled it with a soft kiss.

Next, we are being led over to a fancy cardboard box with metallic coating. Two matching champagne flutes marked 'S & J' are retrieved alongside a bottle of champagne,

'To our new home!' And as the cork is popped, I feel myself bouncing around the room.

Cold clashing with heat

and then that's me gone.

The smoke is here,

with a tight schedule.

It's painful.

I'm burning.

I am plummeting

too fast.

A bang

and—

I land roughly, tripping over my new ankles as I fall to the ground. It takes a moment to realise where I am —

'Oi you lot!' The scattering of school shoes. Pop music plays in these ears but hands rush to pause it.

'Are you alright pet?' We are being lifted by an older woman with hair so perfectly styled it must have taken hours, but it wasn't all that fashionable.

'Those wee brutes don't know what they're at, maybe one of them fancies you?' Our cheeks heat up against the cold. I search for the source of the smoke and realise it's come from a banger. Someone's thrown a firework our way. The smoke is long gone but there's a pain in this chest that lingers like disappointment.

'Eh pretty cutty like you.' She was still talking. In default mode words come out as 'thank you' and 'yes' and 'I really have to go.' These ankles feel no pain as they rush along, this girl's body is refreshingly young. The music is playing again and we keep walking until we're in a house and there's a pot of soup being heated on the hob.

Suddenly I am looking at a phone screen, finally seeing the camera footage of a teenage girl with long hair. Her young fingers are moving faster than I thought possible,

Why'd you throw the banger? You didn't reply all weekend

Don't be a dose about it was just messing. I can feel the memories of a kiss. A messy shift in the middle of a teenage disco. Far too much tongue and ridiculously wet but her chest is full of longing.

Well don't be a dick about it. The fingers hesitated whilst typing this message, switching out 'dick' for 'mean' for 'horrible' for 'dick' again. We glance over at the bubbling soup.

I take control and set the phone down but then it pings again and of course is lifted.

Ha Enda was right you are a clingy bitch- The end of the message is difficult to read because the view is obstructed by tears. The ongoing pop music is switched out for a moody ballad and now we're pacing the room. She spends ages typing then not typing. Crossing between apps and looking through profiles. A picture of her and, presumably, this guy from not even a week ago is at the top of her page. She is wearing a party dress and looks much older than she does in her school uniform. The cub is significantly taller but equally as young, he doesn't smile in the photograph but holds a smug sort of face that says,

'Look who I've pulled.'

       I hear it before I smell it – the smoke alarm made sure.

                Pixelated

                                   grey squares.

All different shades
morphing together to   clog up airways
   making the room reek

                of

                 long

                     lost

                         food

The window is opened,   we escape to the sky,
                the pixels and I.

Now it's pure smoke that tickles all the same but smells so much better. It's melted wax and buttercream icing, things to anticipate rather than things to forget.

       The smoke clears quickly.

'C'mon now, make a wish.' Seven candles have just been blown out. My vision goes black, these eyes are tightly shut. I think I feel their heart floating, filling up with imaginary helium that's really just hope. This body is impossibly light, like it could never feel physical pain.

'What did you wish for pet?' Before they can reply, a man speaks,

'Aye he wants a woman so he does, wee player so he is!' We are facing the table now as his head curls in on itself. A joking Dad perhaps?

'Your uncle is just teasing; don't you pay him any heed.' Not that then. She places a wrapped present beside the cake. Immediately tiny little fingers are ripping at the paper, revealing a plastic toy of some sort, maybe a car. In the reflection of the protective plastic screen, I see a boy grinning. He begins the process of opening the box.

'Now it's only something wee since Santy is coming so soon.' His head turns from the present to look at her,

'How will he know we've moved, Mum?'

'Well, he's Santa, he knows everything, might even visit you at your Dad's too.' I am faced with the present again, a truck? Maybe it's a – now I see his Mum again,

'So double the presents?' I want to laugh but our lips stay taut. The uncle steals my thoughts,

'That's the boy, rinse him clean.' His Mum shoots a dirty look but answers the question nonetheless,

'Well yeah I guess so.' He continues opening the fire engine with less vigour. She pushes,

'Have you got your list ready?' The present is forgotten as he bolts upstairs, hoking through a drawer full of messy sheets pulling out a page with multicoloured writing, all misspelled of course. He's back down in the living room in a second, obediently laying out the list per his uncle's request. The uncle sighs, prompting the wee boy to read out his list.

'A paint set, a toy tractor and a digital-' his words blur into each other as he speed-reads the rest but then just at the end he throws in,

'A beach day with Mum and Dad.' The adults exchange a look as I feel his eyebrows wriggle up to his hairline.

'Well that's quite the list, Santa will try his best but don't expect everything.' His eyebrows are settled but now his heart has drooped down to his feet.

Still, they toss the list into the fireplace and we have full view as it ignites.

As the letters disperse into smoke, I wave goodbye to the elf on the rooftop.

I grin,
        tiptoeing to the clouds.
Settling for a minute,
            the fake fluffs blur into one.
The smoke ballerinas are resting backstage,
                the matted wool a knitted scarf,
            all the buildings just little pixels.
        I bow to the atmosphere
    and greet every bird
as I mimic their wings and fly back down to earth.
I am back on my hill. I look out at the sea of smoke
before beginning my descent. The old man's chimney
is still pumping out smoke, the bonfire depleted by the
recent rain, the firework long gone and the elf off to their
own home. As I clamber down the hill I focus on my steps,
staring intently at each thorny weed and cluster of sheep
manure.

I block out my newly stolen memories as I use a
firelighter to energise the ashes of my abandoned flames,
strategically stacking twigs. I sit in silence as I wait for the
fire to reach a heat that burns my calves from a half a foot
away. It takes its time as my eyes become irritably dry.

Finally, I let the tears fall. The grief, the fear, the
disappointment, and the confusion all hit me at once and
come together to create an absolutely suffocating sense
of loneliness. The feeling I had a struggled to pinpoint all
along. The reason for my excessive sleeping and my corner
shop nattering. Loneliness.

Almost, but Not Quite

by Grace Wilson McNeal

Grace is a full-time student, who enjoys creative writing as part of her English degree. She has been writing since she was young, her love of storytelling initiated on long walks with her family during which she would relay her imaginative tales to her parents.

There's a hole in the floor in the kitchen. It watches me whilst I'm making tea. Its edges are smooth and clean, the lines between the splotchy blue-grey lino and the hole's rim running neatly parallel, as though it had been installed by the workmen from IKEA when they'd come to do the splashback. It is round, but not perfectly round, the sort of imperfect that unsettles you. That looming feeling that you know that something isn't quite right, perhaps not consciously but subconsciously at least, leans into you, an unknown weight resting carefully on the back of your neck. And that 'knowing-but-not-quite-knowing' sits in the back of your mind like the uninvited guest at a party that sits in the corner of the room. Watching. Just like the hole as it watches me fill the kettle.

'Two sugars, please!' Lizzie had let herself in the front door. A loud thump caused me to spill milk across the counter, followed by muttered swearing and 'Sorry!' She'd knocked over the new umbrella stand on her way in, again. I smirked, mopping up the puddle of white with a fresh jay-cloth.

'Don't worry about it!' I replaced the milk in the fridge and added the sugars to one of the mugs. Lizzie rarely had time to grab breakfast before she left her house, two streets over, so her mornings at college tended to be fuelled by caffeine and toothpaste. But she always made time for tea at mine before we walked in together. The floorboards in the hall creaked as she padded past the stairs towards me. She grinned at me through ripples of golden freckles. The corners of her mouth lifted, scrunching slight lines along her nose and pushing the apples of her cheeks upwards, glowing rosy with the thin layer of sunburn that joined across the straight bridge above her nostrils.

'Still there then?' She nodded to the hole as she entered the kitchen, letting her bag slide slowly off her shoulder

until it fell floorward, catching it in her hand just before
laying it to lean against the cracked paint at the bottom of
the doorframe.

'Yeah...still there. Still weird.'

'Have you got anyone in to look at it yet?' I slid the mug
I'd added sugar to across the counter. Lizzie took it and
raised it to her mouth, her lips parted slightly to blow. She
watched the steam curl outwards and spill over the edges
of the cup, examining the minor disruption caused by her
breath.

'I, err—'

'What do you think's down there?' she chimed before I
could answer the question. It was an obvious question, one
that had been hanging quietly in the air since last Thursday
when the hole first appeared. It was now Monday morning,
and that question remained mostly unanswered. Mostly.
Lizzie had not taken her eyes off the hole since she'd got
here, and as she carefully sipped her tea, I couldn't help but
look too. We stood in silence for a few moments, staring
at the floor in the corner, or rather lack-there-of. It stared
back at us. The fridge hummed gently.

'I really don't know... come on, we're going to be late.'

The air outside felt harder than usual, as though
the oxygen had been frozen overnight by winter's grip.
Breathing made my chest ache, the cold reaching down my
throat and squeezing my lungs until I exhaled, causing the
hands to relinquish their hold. Lizzie and I stomped side by
side, our hands in our pockets, chatting about the weather
and college and what shade of pink my business studies
professor would be wearing today. She was just beginning
to explain to me the difference between 'baby pink' and
'light pink' when I saw him. Lizzie trailed off mid-sentence,
noticing my slowed pace and breaking her focus from the
pavement. She looked up to catch the concern on my face

and followed my gaze to the other side of the road. I'd stopped, eyes fixed on the figure across from us.

His skin was almost as pale as the frost that lined the windows of the cars parked along the roadside, pulled tightly around his face as if it were pinned in place. The top of his head was concealed by a grey fedora, tilted low over his forehead so that his eyes were only just visible; I couldn't make out the colour from this distance. I could, however, see how low his mouth sat on his chin, slightly ajar. It was as though his waxy complexion had melted slightly, causing his lips to slide too far down. He wore a long brown coat that finished just above his ankles, below which hung his shoes. I say hung, because they were hanging, about two inches above the ground so that the toes almost scraped the concrete. A passerby may have mistaken him as being stood on his tiptoes. His arms hung limply at his sides. Something unknown made me step down off the pavement onto the road. I wanted to get closer.

Lizzie grabbed my arm and pulled me back.

'Stop what are you doing!?' she hissed, dragging me away down the street, walking so fast I kept tripping in my attempt to keep pace. I couldn't help glancing back. He was still there, head turned slightly towards us as we scurried away. Watching.

'What the hell was that?'

'I have no idea.'

I thought about the man all the way through my first lesson. I couldn't get rid of his lifeless expression. However, by Business Studies my attention had wandered to the intrusive shade of fuchsia Ms Ludworth had adorned herself with that morning. I sat at the back next to the window; I liked watching the world go by outside. Ms Ludworth was chatting about her personal life again, somehow drawing relevance between finances and her ex-husband. I drummed my fingers on my textbook, tapping the title with my ring finger. My fingertips walked their way across the letters and onto the desk and then, as if instinctively, dipped into it. It was as though the solidity of the surface had melted away, my hand sliding through the wood as if it were liquid. Cool ripples engulfed the nerves between my knuckles, each individual splinter of wood parting to slot intricately into the creases. Disbelieving, I wiggled my digits. The feeling could be likened to that of putting your hand into wet sand. I was briefly reminded of a holiday to soggy Cornwall when I was young; digging my small fists into the ground and feeling the grains move around them and under my fingernails, sitting on the beach at the edge of the water so that the sea could not quite reach me, the waves always being pulled back at the last moment no matter how great of a run up they had had. This memory was barely recognisable as my own now.

I glanced around; no one else seemed to have noticed. My hand was now inserted into the wood up to my wrist. I leant down to peer underneath the desk, expecting to see my fingertips poking through the underside. The surface remained undisturbed, other than a few pieces of dried chewing-gum clinging to the corners.

The bell rang signalling the end of the lesson, causing me to jump and whack my head on one of the metal legs. Embarrassed, I quickly collected my things and scurried out of the door.

'No way.' We had sat in the college canteen today, as it was too cold to sit outside for lunch.

'I know it sounds insane, but I swear it happened. I could feel it, it was just so...strange.' Lizzie was frowning at me through a mouthful of crisps. I was trying to explain to her how I'd defied the laws of physics in my previous lesson. Even as I relayed the incident, I began to doubt whether it had really happened at all. Perhaps I had fallen asleep during Ms Lulworth's explanation of the 'Boston Matrix'. Perhaps I had dreamt it. But it had felt so real. 'Anyway, are we going to talk about that man–' I paused midsentence. 'Are you alright?'

Lizzie had her eyes closed. It appeared she had been listening to me moments before, but she wasn't moving, nor saying anything. Nor looking.

'Lizzie...Lizzie? Lizzie!' I leant towards her, taking her shoulder and shaking it slightly. She did not respond. I glanced around again, wondering if this time someone would have noticed. And that's when I realised just how quiet it was. The people on the table next to us were sat silently, like Lizzie, with their eyes shut. As I looked about us, I realised that no one else in the room had their eyes open. It was as if the whole canteen had short-circuited, every pupil subsequently losing power. The stillness lifted the comforting blanket of familiarity from the surrounding space, revealing a harsh, oppressive starkness that exposed me as a bystander. The lack of noise was disturbing.

'He-...hello?' I was too stunned to form a fluid sentence. 'What?'

I jolted, startled by the unexpected response. Lizzie gawped at me over the table. Her eyes were open once again. The rest of the canteen had resumed, chatter flooding the empty air, softening the atmosphere, everything just as it had been before. I blinked hard, as though forcing my eyelids closed would somehow dislodge the bizarreries of the day from my memory.

'Are you alright?' She had continued eating, oblivious to what I had just witnessed.

'Yeah...yeah. Fine.' Maybe I'd imagined it. I decided that attempting to explain what had just happened was more complicated than just pretending it hadn't happened.

Besides, it was probably safer to keep it to myself. For now.

'You sure? You just seem...different today. I don't know.' She shook her head and shrugged.

'Yeah. I'm fine.'

The mild warmth of the day had slightly thawed the ground, the fresh earthiness of the air making its way between my lips and filling my mouth and nose with the taste of the early evening. I was halfway back to my house, walking alone, when the ghostly glow off the pavement caught my attention. Shades of sapphire filled the sky and stretched across the expanses, forcing the cornflower-coloured daytime back behind the horizon. As my gaze followed the different shades of blue towards the sun, they intensified. Rather than the usual pinks and oranges that bled into the night, the sunset was shrouded in cerulean and cobalt. Blue light had plunged the world into a strange ocean. It reflected off the leaves that swam in the wind, like fishes, as they were blown across my path. The icy luminescence complimented the cool November weather; I was submersed in oddity, half expecting to float in the watery light and be carried the rest of the way down my street. The sun itself was most intriguing, a rich royal blue orb, central to the beautiful chaos of the unfamiliar sky. People were coming out of their houses now, pointing, taking pictures, and as I drifted down my garden path, I was comforted with the knowledge that it was not just me who could see what was happening. I stepped through my front door and carefully closed it, watching the blue beams sneak back behind the wood as I shut myself into the quiet of the hallway.

I tossed my bag down. The house felt soft and bland, pale-yellow walls contrasting with the iridescent reflections of the blue sunset outside. I walked across the floorboards and into the kitchen. Two empty mugs sat atop the counter.

A drip of tea had etched its way down the side of the ceramic and dried in a tiny pool just at the point where the cup met the marble surface top. The fridge hummed gently.

I sat down at the edge of the hole and slid my legs past the perimeter. Time to go home.

Am I Mad?

By Martin Fawcett

Born in Bradford but now residing in Huddersfield, Marty has a young family. In the past, he has struggled with his mental health, namely depression. After he spent time in hospital with a diagnosis of psychosis he decided to re-assess his life and thus has turned to being more creative. Turning his hand to writing, poetry & stand-up comedy. He hopes to get people laughing and then talking about mental health more freely.

Part 1

Am I mad? I think I am. Or at least I am *going* mad. All I want to do is escape! For fear of misunderstanding me, I want to explain. I don't want to escape as in *escape* escape. No, I want to go on living. Just like how a helpless dormouse wants to escape the uncompromising clutch of a hungry kestrel. Despite now, there being a considerable distance to the safety of the ground. Even on the ground, as the earthworm - that is cut in two by the blade of a spade - tries to escape separately back to the darkness of the soil, so too, its life expectancy is somewhat shortened.

What am I to do? If I escape, I could fall quite hard. If I escape, I will surely leave behind something of myself. My former self.

My family will understand eventually. They certainly don't care at this moment in time.

Not one of my sisters have come to see me for months, nor my mum or dad. No phone calls or messages. Nothing! I've seen on social media that my dad had visited with his new girlfriend; he had picked up my sisters and they all went for a meal at a nice little gastro pub. To get there, they had to drive past my house. I mean what sort of shitty thing to do is that?

Truth be told, I wouldn't have wanted to go anyway. I can't stand the man. But I am right, aren't I? To be slightly bitter about being left out?

My mum is always out on the lash with her new fella. That and the fact that she opted to support my ex-wife when we decided to go our separate ways. Well ... when I decided to go *my* separate way.

My mother did a round trip of around 200 miles to visit my ex-wife and at the time I was literally living on the next street. Did she pay her only son a visit? No, did she balls! Even now, even though I only live 10 minutes away, she doesn't visit. Not even to see her grandchildren!

As I stand in this little triangular outcrop of trees thinking about the size of tarpaulin I need, I can hear you. 'You have children!' Do you think that I don't know that? If it weren't for my children, I would have escaped a long time ago. Quite simply, they are the only ones holding me back.

My children deserve more from me, I am not being what I am supposed to be. A dad. I am miserable constantly, I'm no fun to be around and I feel like I'm constantly on their back over the most minute of things. When they come to me with their stories or problems, I'm telling them that I'm not interested. If I'm not telling them it, then I am at least thinking it. I should be better.

Truth is, I'm not interested. I'm far from it. I just want to be left alone and I want my responsibilities to disappear. It's not that I don't love them either, that's not it at all. It's because I love them that deep down, I know they deserve more but right now, I can't give them more.

Sure, the guilt is absolutely crippling me and there's been many moments where I've just broken down in tears. In private of course. Nobody will see my tears. Nobody will see that I am struggling.

It is quite nice out here though. I found myself a little wooded area with the trees providing some decent natural shelter. There's a little beck running down one side of it for drinking water, and I've even seen a few pheasants knocking about in an adjacent field. I reckon with a bow and arrow of some kind, or even a slingshot, I could easily kill one when I get hungry. Docile fuckers.

I never chose to live this life; I was never given a choice. My current life just feels like a trade-off.

You see, I believe that everyone has a right to shelter, food and water. I believe everyone has a right to live in peace and without fear. Everyone has a right to enjoy their lives. All those things don't have to be earned through hard work or inheritance; all those things should just exist for everyone. Yet I find myself in a constant struggle with them all.

Of course, I know I'm not the worst off, but I really struggle knowing that others are struggling too, and I can't do fuck all about it. All over the world there is misery. Lots of it.

If I manage to escape and create a life free of restriction imposed on me from 'society' or those in authority, then surely, I will be living in a world completely different to the one I wish to depart?

None of us can see tomorrow, but I sure as hell can see yesterday.

Am I mad? To you ... probably.

Part 2

Jesus Christ! What's with all the pop ups on my phone? Are you doing this? Spamming me into submission so that I buy a god damn Google phone? I don't want one, so stop it! By the way, Jesus was *just* a man. That's right, *just* a man. Nothing more, nothing less.

Last week, have a guess what the news bulletin chose as their last article? Not even a guess? Well, I'll tell you. There was nothing about the atrocities occurring in Yemen at the hands of the Saudis who are being supported by western governments and additionally being supported by weapons being made right here in the UK. There was nothing about our Defence Secretary justifying the permits for the sale of such weapons because they *help* keep the UK public employed. In the entire bulletin not a word about any of this.

So, I'll ask again. What news story did they run as their last article?

You're supposed to at least have a guess!

Well, I'll tell you... A cobbler had lost his thumb during a work-related accident and so he had it replaced with his big toe!

That man can carry on cobbling whilst *innocent* people elsewhere can die *needlessly* without ever being heard.

What am I going to do about it? Well, you're listening to what I'm saying, so you tell me! I'm just merely pointing out the injustice and lack of coverage. There are no *stitching* lives back together for everyone is there?

I'm glad you agree.

I'm making a brew, are you coming with me?

I wonder how efficiently I can make this coffee? I'm pretty sure that I can refine the coffee making process, which would then give me more time to do other things, like ... thinking.

Step 1, Water in and kettle on. Step 2, Sugar, coffee and milk in. Step 3, pour water and stir. Done.
Impressive. I know!

1, 2, 3. 1, 2, 3.

You are right. There is some pattern to it isn't there? 1, 2, 3.

That's it! Head, heart and gut.

All decision making is done via the head, heart and gut. Often, it's a combination of 2 or more. But... what if you've lost your head? If you lose that then the head can't interpret the heart. Then you're left with the gut and whilst following your gut works sometimes, it's not good if you've only got your gut to guide you through everything... is it?

Easy as 1, 2, 3. Wait a minute!

That's where the saying comes from? That's the order in which every decision should be made? Check your head, then your heart? Failing those two, go with your gut? Well blow me down sideways.

I need to switch the kettle off at the mains?

I see. It's a test.

You little sly dog. Well, this is easy. I'll use 1, 2, 3. Off, on, off, on, off.

There you go. Switched off on the third go. Head, heart & gut! All bases covered. You thought I wouldn't get it. You underestimate me. Aha!

That's enough now anyway, I need to go to the shop for more coffee.

My gut is telling me not to walk the same way back home, what do you think? Follow my instinct?

I'll put my headphones in, but I won't have anything playing so that I can still hear you, so don't worry. If anyone says anything about me, I'll be able to hear it.

Nobody is following us... that's good. Hold on... why is that guy just sat in that van there? Virgin media don't work at this time, do they? It's like almost 10 at night! There's something fishy about him.

Alright then, I'll do that. Let's see what he says.

How could he not have a brochure? How? Something isn't right with him like. I'm walking a different way back home. If he follows, we'll see him.

Ooh yes, I'll get a fancy coffee. Splash out a little.

You're too funny you. How on earth do I do that?

Just say it as though it's normal? I don't think I can do that. It's not normal to randomly give lyrics to someone serving you, normally you'd ask for a carrier bag or something.

Alright, alright I'll think of something. Good god!

Bahahaha! She must have thought that I'm off my nut!

'What bridge? Troubled water?' That was hilarious!

I kept a straight face though, did you see? I know, I know. It's just a bit of harmless fun.

Hold on a minute. That virgin media van has gone. Keep an eye out for it. *Yes*, I will do as well.

Why is Andrew Neil looking at me like that? Its freaking me out a bit. Talking all in riddles and then looking at me through the screen as though I should know what he's on about. Well, I don't! Nobody bloody knows what he's on about. Not even Michael Portillo knows what he's on about. Andrew Neil ha! You knobhead!

Wait what?! He can fucking hear me!

He's just heard me call him a knobhead! Look! He's laughing at me! I don't understand. How?

Telepathy? Go away! I'm not telepathic. Hold on, hold

on.

No fucking way! He's telling me to piss off in his riddles! This is insane! Well, I have to say, this is both weird and quite impressive. What else can I do?

Time travel?

Fuck off. Prove it.

No. You'll have to pick somewhere. My head is spinning.

1985? Why then? Live Aid? Yes, I know it. No, he didn't. No, I'm not buying that at all.

Wait, how does it work exactly? Uh, huh. Uh, huh. So, my body can stay here? That doesn't sound too scary then. Come on then. Let's do it!

WHOOOA!

THIS...

IS...

FUCKING...

INSAANNNEEEE!

Oh my sweet, sweet Freddie. Hey! Can you see what I'm

seeing?

The queen himself is singing to me! How on earth did you get me this spot? This is the most incredible thing ever! Wow! Look at all those people. There's got to be millions!

Wait a minute... Are they all singing to me too? Why?

I've been chosen. Chosen for what?

To eradicate misery and suffering from the world. How on earth am I going to do that? With the help of good people. What people?

Me? I'm not the second messiah, no way! A god? Not a chance! Bring me back now, I need to get some fresh air. This is far too much for anyone to take.

Just leave me alone now please, I need to walk in peace. I need to take all this in. I need to try get my head around understanding what all this means.

No wait! No! I haven't had enough time yet. Look, I'm in the middle of a fucking wood and I'm exhausted. I'm in no position yet to be giving you an answer as to whether I want to *save the world* or not.

What do you mean that it's easy? I need to transition? What does that even mean? This is mental! I can't decide right now.

I can't! I mean, I would love to save the world but surely, I don't have to be a god to do that? Don't worry? A team? Supporting me? Join a world that parallels the one I exist

in right now? You mean escape to a different world? Well …
I can sort of get my head around that; it's just I would have
thought that I could do that in a different way. Not for one
minute did I imagine anything like this. So, forgive me for
wanting to take some time.

Right … okay.

What do I do?

Where's that countdown coming from? Can you hear
that? Why can I hear a countdown in my head?!

Hello?

Hello! You can't disappear on me now. Why the hell is
there a countdown in my head? What happens when it gets
to zero?
I'm starting to panic now. You can see that I'm panicking
and you're doing nothing! You're saying nothing!

This is freaking me out big time. I'm running from a
countdown in my head and try as I will, I can't escape it.
And you're ignoring me. Of all the times to stop.

Stop! Stop it now! Stop ignoring me! Please, I'm scared!

Don't fight it? Fuck you!

I'm going to be reborn. What the hell are you on about?

Don't go fucking quiet on me again! What the fuck do
you mean I'm going to be reborn? I'm going to die, aren't I?
Answer me you prick! Am I going to die?

No. No. No. Nooooooo!

Part 3

Well, it appears that I made it out of the other side.
I've met with these two police officers who turned up out
of nowhere and they've brought me to some place I don't
know. I assuming it's our base of operations.

I have it on good understanding that I'll have everything
I need here. I'll want for nothing, and I'll be kept safe until
the world is made better under my instruction.

But before I enter there seems to be some final test that
I must pass. I guess it's just extra security measures. You
know, just to make sure I am who I say I am.

This official looking dude has been in and out a few times
now. 'Who are you?' he keeps asking. I keep telling him, but
of course this is a test, so I play it cautiously. See. He's back
again.

To be honest, it's starting to get a bit annoying now.
He's definitely figuring something out. It's not that hard to
understand.

For fuck's sake, why is he leaving again?

Whilst he's gone, let's talk about earlier. That was
some insane ride, wasn't it? When I opened my eyes and
breathed out my first breath, it really was like being reborn
again. My brain literally felt like it had flipped! When we
counted back up to 10 ... I mean, wow. Just wow! So much

power! I've never felt anything like it.

Ah, finally! He's back!

'Who am I?'

Is this guy for real? I don't know who he is. That's a fair point, I don't know him. Is he one of the good guys? What shall I say?

I know. I'll just tell him that he is.

Simple right? If he is and I am, then we are equals. Right?

Surely, he will understand that?

Why the fuck is he looking so confused now?

Jesus Christ! That's right! Fuck off and leave again!

I tell you what though, this little snack box they've given me isn't half bad. A savoury cheese sandwich, a granny smith, a packet of cheese & onion crisps and aside from a fresh orange juice in this poxy little container thing, it's pretty decent.

Oh! The official looking dude is back.

Is he taking the piss now? He is, isn't he?

Why the fuck doesn't *he* tell *me* where we are? I haven't got a bastard clue, but he clearly has! Why is he asking me that?!

Whoops! I think he knows I'm pissed off now.

Thank God! They're taking me to my room in a minute. They're just getting it ready.

So ... erm ... that long haired dude playing the guitar is surreal. Is he playing that for me? I mean, it's a grand welcome. Something isn't right though, is it?

Am I going mad?

Why is she dressed like a nurse? And why are there so many rooms?

No, this doesn't feel right to me. Hello? Talk to me then.

Is this my room?

Why are there hundreds of cigarette burns all over the floor? There are no doors on the wardrobe. I haven't even been given a key. This is not a place fit for a God. What is this place? Hello?

Why are you so quiet all over again?

Hold on a minute, those windows don't look right to me either.

What the hell! My windows have fucking cages on them! In fact, the windows don't even open!

This isn't right this. No. This is *not* right at all!

I'm not meant to be here! I can't be here!

I need to ESCAPE!
This is fucking MADNESS!

Seawater

By Alison Nuorto

An EFL Teacher living in Bournemouth but with a nomadic heart that yearns to roam far and wide. She feasts on horror stories and the traditional ghost stories of M.R. James and harbours an appreciation for the macabre. Her poems have appeared in a handful of anthologies and she was delighted to make the shortlist for the Bournemouth Writing Prize in 2021. Currently, she is working on producing an anthology of her own, to promote awareness of male suicide. As long as she has a pulse, she hopes to always keep writing.

I'm a husk;

All lashed kernel and hollowed hubris.

Hewn from the withering vine.

But plunge me in seawater and I'll shine like the newly presented babe;

Birthed from the core.

Propelled to Galilee,

My shedding will lead to salvage.

The Not So Funny Man
by Deirdre Crowley

Deirdre Crowley is an artist and writer from Bandon Co. Cork, Ireland. Her stories have been published in The Irish Times, The Ogham Stone, The Southern Star, and The Well Short Story Competition. In 2017, she was one of twelve writers short listed for The Sunday Business Post Short Story Award Short. In 2018 she was longlisted for FISH Memoir Prize. In 2019 she was selected for Cork World Book Festival Pitch with an Agent event. In the same year her work was Longlisted and Highly Commended in the Sean O Faolin Short Story Contest.

Last night I dreamt that there was a black horse in my bed. It is a single bed these days by the way, like all the other ones here. Sometimes I try not to remember my dreams, but this one seemed okay. The black horse kept on standing up, repositioning himself and lying down again, as if he was figuring out what was most comfortable. I was standing next to him wondering why he seemed to like putting his silky mane on the three pillows I usually slept on. I was thinking, *Surely that cannot be comfortable for him with his long nec*, but this horse did not seem to mind. I did not intervene with suggestions to him. Once he had settled, he looked like he would start reading one of the books near my reading lamp. I could hardly ask him to leave; he looked so comfortable. Maybe he was the kind of horse who liked to read in bed just like me.

*

The dream reminded me of my dog, the way she used to love to jump up on my double bed when we lived in the cottage. I loved my dog, but I drew the line at her being in my bed or on my bed. (She was half collie and half something else smart. We had chosen each other at the rescue centre. We bothhad wanted a new life.) The only time I would have made an exception to the rule was the night The Not So Funny Man came to stay at my house. I had not invited him; he just seemed to arrive. I had met him and his friend, The Funny One, on a train journey that summer. I was sitting at one of those four seats with a table. I had wanted to sleep and not talk to anyone, but when the train broke down halfway into our journey, conversation started automatically and never stopped for the next hour. The Funny One made me laugh a lot. He had been an actor when younger and now wrote plays for his local dramatic company. They were travelling home after the funeral of a classmate. Arriving at my destination, mobile numbers were exchanged only out of politeness.

'If you're ever up our way,' The Funny One said. 'Me and my wife will treat you to afternoon tea, nothing fancy, just a bit of china and theatrics.'

It all seemed quite harmless. The Not So Funny One insisted on carrying my bag off the train. Other passengers looked at me disapprovingly. A peck on the cheek from both men on the platform must have seemed like I was saying goodbye to my two grandfathers.

*

Weeks later The Not So Funny One phoned me to tell me that his brother had died. I offered my sympathy. He went on to explain how his brother's wife had shut him out. He said that she would not allow him say goodbye to his brother. I remembered how on the train The Funny One had confided in me that The Not So Funny One had a very bitter split from his wife, and how none of his children spoke to him anymore. Just as he was about to say more, The Not so Funny One came back from the buffet carriage with drinks and chocolate. Maybe if The Funny One had been able to tell me more, I would have acted differently.

*

The next phone call I got from the Not So Funny one, was late one gloomy September evening. He said he was in the area and would it be okay if he called to say hello. I was surprised that he had remembered where I lived. As part of the conversation on the train, I had told them that I lived near a tiny village close to the sea. At the time neither of them seemed to know of it. They both lived over a hundred kilometres away. We may as well have been living in different countries.

'I'm really tired, I can only stay a while,' he seemed to be whispering wearily down the phone.

I stuttered that I might be going out, but realised it was

too late. He had hung up.

I had barely time to put on my shoes and jumper when I heard a car crunch onto the gravel. I wondered how he had found me so easily without me giving clear directions. Visitors usually got lost, even with my detailed advice on how to get to me. The twisty roads and turnoffs were easily confused, especially in the dark. I got lost myself some nights.

I opened the glass porch door, as the car headlights dazzled me and my dog. She was barking, instantly annoyed at his arrival. He got out of the car quickly, his eyes shining wildly, his white hair dishevelled and wiry. He looked like someone I had seen in a play once, his bony features waxy from the sensor light.

He opened the back door of the car, taking out flowers and a parcel wrapped in brown paper. On the threshold he presented them to me saying,

'Now, girl, they're for you.' The way he said 'girl' made me shiver. Rolling the word slowly off his tongue, he made it sound vulgar. Walking past me he went for the kitchen, like he knew where it was. He seemed to be moving faster than I had remembered. I paused at the door, feeling like someone was trespassing; it took me a while to follow him into the kitchen. I offered him tea as he walked around admiring everything and me.

'It's so good to see you,' he said, squeezing my shoulders as I filled the kettle in the sink. His fingers felt claw-like, his breath sounded heavy near my neck.

'Ouch!' he shouted. 'You little bitch.'

My dog had nipped him on the heel.

I apologised and gave a pretend scold to my dog who was panting at my knee. She was doing her stressed yawning, something I saw her do rarely. It usually happened at the vets, or if we were in places that were too crowded or around people she thought too loud. She was standing rigid next to me like she was stuck in cement. When he turned his back, I rubbed her ear. She licked my sweaty wrist, yet neither of us relaxed.

'I'm exhausted,' The Not So Funny Man said, flattening his thin hair down as he sat at the kitchen table. Stretching out his long legs and exposing bare hairy ankles, he was sockless in his polished brown brogues. His laces were untied too.

He glanced quickly over his shoulders as if checking to see if anyone might be listening.

'I don't think I can drive home tonight. I just might stay here,' he said emphatically. 'I haven't been sleeping well, you know!'

He was bowing his head now over his cup. His hands seemed to tremble as he held the steaming tea. This gesture made him seem smaller, almost vulnerable. His eyes looked bloodshot. It had not occurred to me that he might have been drinking.

'I know it's late,' he said. 'It is so nice to see you, and I can see you are happy to see me too.' He licked his lips and nodded as if agreeing with himself.

'That's it decided then, I'll stay tonight and be gone first thing in the morning.'

He was staring at me now, his look intimidating.

'Yes, yes of course,' I said far too quickly. 'I have a spare room for visitors.'

I really wanted to add that usually my visitors were invited and did not just land out of nowhere in the dark and that my dog had never nipped anyone before, not even the postman.

I poured more tea from the white ceramic tea pot I had bought when I moved into the cottage. It was a symbol of my new clean life. I had hoped that I might become a minimalist someday, with everything white and tidy. I had rented the place on my own after two break- ups. One was devastating and the other just another mistake. Initially the cottage had given me time to heal, but recently I was glad I had only signed a one-year lease. I did not know how I would survive a winter there. There were too many crows in the trees nearby. Sometimes it seemed that collectively they could block out the sky. Other times they made so much noise I had to keep the windows shut. Lately I could hear them cawing in my head, even when sleeping.

The Not So Funny Man was smiling at me now. He seemed to be about to reach out and touch me.

'I've run out of milk,' I said in a panic, jumping up quickly. My dog moved with me. The thought of having to talk to him for longer was making me queasy.

'I'll drive to the village,' he said, clapping his hands.

'In fact, we can both go and have a drink in the pub while we're there. It is a nice little pub. They know all about you there.'

I felt myself go hotter. I had never been in the local pub; there were always men outside smoking. They would stare at my car as I drove past, early or late, it did not matter. At weekends, teenage girls in short dresses and young boys in T-shirts huddled around the entrance smoking and laughing, waiting for the bus to take them to the neighbouring town nightclub. Sometimes one or two would be vomiting at the side entrance under the yard light. On Sunday mornings there were always plastic glasses and chip wrappers blowing around the road like tattered ghosts from the night before. The woman who ran the pub had dyed black frizzy hair and big teeth. I would see her standing in the door with the smoking men and teenagers laughing one minute, glaring at passing traffic the next. She always seemed to be wearing white jeans and tops. I wondered how she would keep them clean if she was pulling pints. Maybe someone else was doing that for her. The girl in the shop said she was great for the village. She said if it wasn't for her they would have nothing, especially the teenagers, they had nowhere else to go.

That place was the last place I wanted to go.

'No, no,' I replied. 'You stay here, and I'll be back in no time.''Don't worry,' he said. 'We don't need to go to the pub, I have a bottle of wine in the car for you too. I'll wait until you come back to open it.''No,' I insisted. 'I don't drink wine.' I had not taken a drink in a long time. It was my way of breaking from the habits that in the past had made me fall. I had lost friends because I did not like drinking anymore.

'You're not much fun,' one friend said.

'You've just become boring,' another scolded.

I did not know which was better, having friends like that who told you exactly what they thought, or getting rid of friends like that. It was hard to accept that people I had liked once no longer wanted to be with me.

I gathered my coat and bag and went to leave. I could not find my phone. I was convinced I had left it in the kitchen. It did not seem to matter now that I was getting away from The Not So Funny Man. He stood at the door waving. 'Don't be long now, we'll have a nice chat when you get back.'

Smiling, he closed the door.

My dog barked all the way to the village. She had never barked like that; being in the car was always something that she liked. It was nearly ten o clock; I knew the village shop would be closed. The woman from the bar stood in the doorway and gave me an unsettling wave as I drove by. *What did she know about me*, I wondered?

I drove on to the town, not sure where would be open,

half convincing myself that I did need milk after all. It was comforting to be in a place with streetlights. I could call Yvonne, but she would probably be in bed with her husband. She had visited me once or twice, but I had never been officially invited back to her place. It was a Tuesday night, a back-to-school feel made the poorly lit houses seem joyless. What would I say to Yvonne anyway? There is an old man staying in my house tonight and I am afraid to stay there now?Yvonne was a new friend that I had made at the weekly farmers' market. The cakes and scones I baked were popular with the Saturday shoppers. She made fudge; she swore she never ate it herself as it was too sugary. The other stall holders were less friendly. They viewed me with suspicion. Most of them had authoritative accents that sounded like they knew about everything. They would talk to each other loudly in between customers. When we were packing up later, Yvonne and I would laugh at some of the things they would say.

'Where are you from?' the guy from the buffalo mozzarella stall had asked me my first day.

'From out the road,' I replied. 'Ten miles away.'

'Ah, but you're not really from here,' he said. 'You're not local.' He kept on at me, joking yet serious.

He claimed he was local because he had lived in the town for three years.

Yvonne said he was hitting on me. She said he had tried the same tactics with her until he saw her husband. She was convinced he had army background. She said that the knife and boots were a dead giveaway. She accused me of being too shy for my own good. It was something I could not help.

The woman selling organic honey had quizzed me about who had recommended me to the committee of the farmers' market. She asked me where I had trained. I told her that my grandmother had taught me how to bake. Foolishly,

I found myself telling her about how she had raised me too. I do not know why I gave her that information, I must have been nervous. She did not seem remotely interested but raved on about Imelda's cakes next to her stall, telling me that they were all gluten free and organic. Imelda just glared at me. She looked like the least organic person you could imagine. Her face was orange. I wondered if organic carrots made you go that colour. I had read once that carotene was a natural tanning agent.

It was drizzling now as I circled the town looking to see if anywhere was open. My dog had settled down, and in the mirror, I could see her attempting to sleep. I felt drowsy myself. I pulled into the church carpark. Surely with the doors locked we would be safe parked up there for the night? The graveyard residents nearby would keep watch over us.

Then I remembered something my grandmother used to say, it was that a kindness to a stranger could save a life. Why was I being so foolish? The man in my house was only a few years younger than my grandmother had been when she died. I was with her holding her hand. When I had to let it go finally, I remember feeling abandoned for the first time in my twenty-five years of living. Now years later I felt the same aloneness, it came down around me heavy as the dark. I had to push the weight off as a pain dragged across my chest. Deep breathing, I reasoned with myself that the best thing to do would be to head back to the cottage. I had to be up early in the morning to do an order of cakes for a birthday party. My dog would get to sleep on my bed for one night only. Everything would be fine.

Approaching the village, I noticed a dead badger, blood and fur squashed into the ground; further up the road, a headless pigeon. I had not seen these casualties earlier. They were not unusual around here. As the car crawled slowly up the hill to the cottage, my dog awoke and started barking again. The light was on in the guest bedroom, the curtains were pulled, his car was gone, though. I felt relief.

Entering the cottage, a strange musty smell hung in the air. On the kitchen table a bottle of red wine stood open alongside a drained glass. Lifting it, I inhaled the bitter aroma. It was almost empty. My phone lay there, the screen dead to touch. Walking down the hall, I stopped when I got to the guest room. I knocked on the bedroom door and called out. I turned the silver handle, opening it slowly. The bedclothes looked dented. He must have slept for a while and then left. That was all he had wanted, I told myself. Now I worried if he had been fit to drive. I started to shake the pillows and smooth the covers. My dog shot hurriedly to the porch door, scratching it wildly to get out. I followed her. The barking was piercing until I screamed at her to stop. When I opened the door, The Not So Funny Man was standing there saying,

'Where have you been, my love, don't you know I've been waiting all night for you?'

Red wine dripped from his bloodied lips. His wet body raged toward me. Everything went dark. Even the crows were silent, just like me.

The Boy on the Bike

by Henry Tydeman

Henry is an English tutor. In 2021 his short story 'The Pigeons' was shortlisted in the Wild Hunt Magazine prize, and another of his stories was chosen for publication in the Manchester Review. His short plays have been performed by the New Works Playhouse. He has also written about politics and the arts for Huffington Post and Reaction.

The day after Nan died, Charlie started cycling.

When she was in the hospital – he hadn't visited her, the prospect terrified him – he'd wandered about the house without anything to do, unable to relax, troubled by a strange, nervous sadness. He'd been nervous before, on school sports days, and sad (films sometimes made him cry when no one was looking) but never this unsettling combination that made his heart beat fast and his mind ache. He couldn't concentrate on anything else. He'd pick up a book or turn on the television, but within minutes they'd just seem like unwanted distractions. And he wasn't hungry; the sandwiches Dad made were left untouched, forlorn.

He knew that she was dying. His parents had said so. She'd fallen over in her house and banged her head. He would listen to Dad talking on the phone and could tell straight away that he was speaking to Mum because it was his serious voice. There were long gaps when Dad hardly spoke. Charlie would sit in the next room and hear the call end and his father's purposeful footsteps. 'She's sleeping,' he'd say, or 'She's the same as before.' Then, five days after she fell, the footsteps were a little slower and he knew immediately. 'Nan died this morning, Charlie.'

The bike was in the shed. He wheeled it out and stood with it on the pavement in the still air and the quiet. He was surprised at one thing. His feelings hadn't changed since he'd found out. He had expected that an ocean of tears would pour forth like it did in films, that he would cling to his parents, shaking, gasping amidst the flood, but that at least the nervousness would subside. But none of this was right; he hadn't cried and the nerves remained, prickling. What was there to be nervous about now? The bike was another attempt to take his mind off things. He didn't hold out much hope. He'd never cycled in the road before, and so he decided to stick to the pavements. He wouldn't go far, just around the block or along a couple of streets and back. The sky was white and indifferent and hung above like an old sheet or a cheaply painted ceiling. Charlie sat on the seat, gripped the handlebars, and carefully started pedalling. He wobbled, but quickly rebalanced, each of the muscles in his arms and legs doing exactly as they should, as if they had minds of their own, working together like a troupe of dancers in a musical, the end result a fabulous display of human ingenuity, and he was away, chugging over paving stones, negotiating cracks and little bumps here and there. And it felt... good, bracing, the way it engaged the whole body, an all-encompassing activity, the arms and legs and chest which had been weighed down and deadened by unremitting, crude feeling for days were now in motion again and he felt lighter and went faster. The crisp air on his face burrowed in wherever it could and he opened his eyes wider – and even his mouth – as he went along. It seemed to revive him. His clogged mind was a little clearer, and he felt a kind of... calm.

So, he went out on the bike every day, and when he did it always seemed that the sadness and the nerves were somehow crowded out and he stopped noticing them. He started going for longer, and further, wheeling the bike carefully across the roads so he could try new streets, different blocks. Neighbours were cheered by the pleasant, innocent sight of the boy on the bike (though some scowled and felt that cycling should never be allowed on the pavements).

Nan's house was only four streets away. He'd avoided it for the first week, but then, on a damp Monday morning, he found himself there at its end and paused. He thought that it was somehow childish of him to miss out this street deliberately, and so, feeling brave, he turned and began pedalling along the pavement. He was thinking of her as he came up alongside the house. The curtains were closed. There was no light beyond them. The place looked so lonely, like a lost dog, tired of whimpering but still plagued by fear and emptiness.

Charlie felt a rush of vivid emotion in his cheeks and behind his eyes, and quickly – before the tears that he knew were coming – he set off again. All evening he thought of the house, with its blue door and the darkness behind the curtains. He didn't tell Dad, and he realised that as well as the sadness, he felt so sorry for Nan. The same way he felt at school when someone was being picked on. But at school you could say something, or the person could fight back, stick up for themselves; there was a way out, the potential for justice, or consolation at least. It wasn't the same for her.

And yet, he kept on coming back, standing in the same spot and thinking the same things. He remembered all the different rooms, and every time he did, she was there, sat on the sofa or stood up chopping vegetables in the kitchen. Then he'd make himself picture them empty, dust on the surfaces, complete silence. Perhaps there was a half-finished plate of something. And the pity he felt grew, because she'd been unfairly treated – that's how it seemed. Taken away like that, all of a sudden and without warning, halfway through breakfast. It wasn't right. At home he hugged the pillow and imagined it was her. He'd stand outside her place every day and feel the surge coming on, waves of feeling, and yet after a while he could also tell – though he would never have admitted this to anyone – that he was somehow... enjoying it. It was a strange thing. He'd started going out on the bike to get away from all that – and it had worked – yet now he almost craved it, he sought it out, the deep ache, the profusion of feelings, the inevitable tears. There was something about it that he needed, that he went back for. It seemed to satisfy him.

He was standing in the usual spot, the sad house ahead of him, his bike off to one side (he'd started leaning it against a lamppost). He gazed at the bricks, at the windows, at all of it, and the feelings came on as strong as ever. He was basking in them, like a reptile in the sunlight, in the misery he had found that was his own and no one else's, and for a split second he thought that the sun had flashed against the kitchen window. But it hadn't, and Charlie felt his insides suddenly drop away. The light in the kitchen had been turned on. He could see clearly, behind the blinds, strips of yellow. Signs of life.

Charlie was scared. He looked around in the empty street then back up towards the kitchen. The light shone. A burglar. It had to be a burglar. That thought made him angry. It was an outrage! He knew the sensible thing would be to go home and tell Dad, but something drove him on, he hardly stopped to think at all, and up he went to the front door and pushed against it. It was unlocked. He stood in the little porch and listened. Yes, there was definitely someone in the kitchen. He heard the clanging of plates, footsteps and... music. They'd put the radio on! He imagined it was a group of them, and that they were dancing in celebration as they filled their bags with Nan's old cutlery and whatever else took their fancy. Fear and rage mingled inside him. He wanted to run, but he'd never forgive himself if he did. He had to stand face to face with them, for Nan's sake. It was the least he could do. He hoped they'd take one look at him and scarper, and he could say that he'd frightened them off. She'd be so proud.

He crept round the corner and saw where the light from the kitchen spilled out onto the carpet in the hallway. The music was louder. There were no voices. His heart was beating so very fast, he'd already decided to show himself, to shout, or scream, or go for them perhaps, with his fists. He was a foot from the open door. He took a deep breath, tensed, and stepped defiantly into the light, so they could see him, and he opened his mouth to cry out, as loudly as he could.

Nan gasped. Then smiled.

'Oh, it's you.'

Charlie's mouth stayed open. There she was, with her apron on, a big serving spoon in her hand.

'It's shepherd's pie, I know you like shepherd's pie.'

It really was shepherd's pie. He could smell it.

'Have you set the table?'

Charlie went on looking at her. The warm light, the heat from the oven, the shepherd's pie, it all seemed to merge together into one block of extraordinary sensation, he was almost overwhelmed... and yet it made him so very happy, that she was still here, that dinner was almost ready.

But she was dead, wasn't she? She was definitely dead.

'Hug!' he stammered.

'What?'

'Hug!' He went towards her quickly with his arms outstretched, for he longed to hold onto her more than anything, and he knew too that this would be proof, beautiful proof, lasting evidence that the days he'd been living through had been some long, awful dream.

'You are a sweetheart aren't you!'

And sure enough, there she was, all big and warm and laughing at his silliness, wrapping her arms around him tightly.

'I love you, Nan!'

'I love you too, Charlie.'

From where his head was positioned he could see the

scrunched-up tissue she kept up her sleeve. It was pushed up right next to his eyes and he saw all the little folds and tears and details, and he could smell the strange soap she used, the pink block from her bathroom, the type Mum hated.

'But don't think this gets you out of laying the table!'

And so they sat down together to eat, and they talked as they always did, about school, Charlie's parents, something Nan had seen on TV. It was all so wonderfully ordinary. At one moment, a break in the conversation, Charlie looked out through the curtains. He saw the bike against the lamppost and remembered.

'I thought you were a burglar! I saw the kitchen light. I thought it was a robber!'

She finished her mouthful.

'Why did you think that?'

'Because...' he was frowning, confused. 'Because I thought you were dead,' he whispered, looking at her uneasily, guiltily. 'I don't know why.'

She smiled at him caringly, with just a hint, a flicker of sadness. Then, as she pushed another piece of shepherd's pie onto the back of her fork, she said straightforwardly, 'Of course I'm dead, Charlie.'

She popped the food into her mouth. Charlie felt suddenly cold, and there were those nerves again, sparked into life, clawing at his insides like frantic hands.

'What?' he spluttered, 'Don't make jokes!' For a second he hated her.

'Who's joking?' she asked.

'You are!'

'Charlie, don't be silly. You know that I'm dead.' It was as if it was some uninteresting, run of the mill thing. 'I fell over in the kitchen.' She might have been recalling some boring household chore. 'You know all this already.' Then, disapprovingly, 'Don't play the fool.'

He knew, of course, that it was true. He had always known. And then, for the first time, he felt that the tears would really come and there was nothing he could do, and he put his hands to his face as the great surge enveloped him, and shook him mercilessly, so much that he knocked against the table and all the things clattered. She was up immediately and by his side, holding him tightly again, trying to comfort, patting his back and saying, 'There, there,' a little flustered herself, clearly surprised and moved by this sudden turn.

Then they were on the sofa together. Charlie was quiet, tired from crying. Nan spoke gently.

'It happens to everyone, Charlie. You know that.'

He looked straight ahead. He heard his own voice, small and feeble.

'But... I'm still sad. Really sad. All the time.'

'What about when you're riding your bike?' she asked.

He turned towards her.

'How do you know about my bike?'

'Of course I know about you and your bike!'

He folded his arms.

'Well? You're not sad all the time. That's a fib, isn't it Charles. I know you enjoy riding your bike.'

'Most of the time, then. Most of the time I'm really sad.' She had annoyed him by mentioning the bike. She was completely right of course, when he rode the bike he stopped feeling sad, or at least he felt less sad than usual, but here, now, he did not want to be reminded of that. He wanted to stay feeling sad, the depth and the pain of it was somehow reassuring. And he realised he felt guilty at the prospect of happiness.

'There's no need to feel guilty,' she told him.

'I don't...' he started, but stopped.

'When my own mother died, years ago, that's how I felt. I thought about her all the time, every second, it seemed. But sometimes, I'd catch myself thinking about something else. Not thinking about her. And the sadness had stopped, just for a moment. Like a little patch of sun showing through the rain clouds. And immediately I'd feel this awful guilt, as if I'd done something terrible, stopped loving her or something, stopped caring that she was gone. I thought it would upset her. I almost wanted to be sad. Isn't that a silly thing!' She looked at him knowingly over the top of her glasses. 'Wouldn't you agree?'

It did sound silly when she put it like that. But Charlie found that he could not say out loud that he agreed, as if a key had turned and his mouth was locked. To say she was right, the prospect of it almost frightened him.

'Of course, everyone goes through the same sort of thing. It takes a bit of time, and that's alright. After a while you'll be ready, Charlie, don't you worry about that!'

'Ready for what?' he asked quietly. He did not like her calmness in her voice at all. He fidgeted and his mouth wobbled.

She was smiling now, so warm and with such love. 'Ready to be happy again, of course!'

He had started to cry again, though not loudly this time, and he found that he was still able to speak a bit through the tears.

'I just feel sorry for you,' he told her.

And then, peculiarly, she laughed. A short, instinctive laugh. He didn't understand.

'Oh, Charlie! Of course you don't!'

That annoyed him.

'I DO!'

She looked a little more seriously at him.

'No, Charlie. You don't.'

Her response had surprised him so much that he'd stopped crying.

'What...?'

'I haven't broken a bone. Or... had my things stolen by burglars. *Then* you might feel sorry for me. But I'm dead. It's very different. Totally different in fact. I don't exist. You can't feel sorry for someone that doesn't exist. It doesn't make sense.' She was speaking in that matter of fact tone again. 'Think about it.'

Charlie was frowning again. He thought about it. He did feel sorry for her, didn't he?

'You don't,' she insisted.

He considered the examples she'd given, the broken bone and the burglar, and thought of her hobbling about on crutches, or powerless to resist as robbers took all her precious things. Her sad face afterwards. Living through it.

'That's it,' she said, encouragingly.

And then he closed his eyes and tried to think of her now, now that she was dead... but somehow, he could not think of her, or rather he didn't know where to place her, how her face would look, because that was just it, she was gone, she wasn't anywhere. He gasped and opened his eyes.

'The only person you feel sorry for is you, Charlie. And that's alright. After all, it's not a nice thing you've been through. Worse than a broken bone, I'd say!'

All the time she was smiling, and the warm lights in the room seemed soft and beautiful, like an old painting. Charlie sat closer to his grandmother and they put their arms around each other once more. He didn't speak. He was not happy yet. The panging grief was still there, and he missed her terribly. He felt tired. But something had changed. She did not exist, he knew that. And if she did not exist, then she could feel no unhappiness, no fear. So there was no reason, as she'd told him, to feel sorry for her. He did not need to worry about her. He could feel the bump in her sleeve where she always kept that tissue. He even heard her breathing.

And he did feel sorry for himself. Why should he have to go through something as horrible as this? He was only eleven. But, he realised, the nerves that had troubled him through all of those days, the nerves that had worn him out and stopped him eating, they had gone. Like a great flock of birds, disturbed by some sound or change in the air, they'd taken off as one and were far away now, still in view but only just, a million specks on the shoreline, soaring and pulsing. Distant.

Charlie watched them for a moment more, and then turned away.

The Ghost of Charlie Jr

by Jen Hall

Jen is a fundraiser from the West of England. She loves happy TV shows and movies, but prefers books that are heart-breaking. Writing is her passion, exploring darkness and loneliness while wearing cosy socks. One of her stories was published for the first time in 2021.

Charlie Jr died just before dawn on 12th October 1983.
At the end, it was as if he just couldn't face another day of
pain, and tubes, and people holding his hand and crying.
It's one of those weird truths that people put down to
coincidence; most deaths happen just before dawn if you
take out those hit by buses, and all the violence. Deaths at
home and in hospital, where people finally let go, they're
most likely to happen just before dawn.

Charlie Sr knows lots of facts like this. He was a sociology
lecturer. He knows that statistically, a plane that crashes
has more no-shows than planes that land safely. People
don't say they missed the flight because of a bad feeling.
They say their alarm clock didn't go off, they forgot their
passport and had to go back, the car ran out of petrol. All
completely unrelated reasons. But as a whole, they suggest
that people do have some kind of sixth sense. Buried deep
in our subconscious. So deep we are unaware.

And if you believe that, it's not so much of a jump
to believing in ghosts. Charlie Sr wasn't sure that he
did believe in the sixth sense. Even after decades of
undergraduates wide eyed and excited at this 'proof' of a
sixth sense. But when the ghost of Charlie Jr arrived at
his home in the evening of 12th October 1983, Charlie Sr
thought he had better start believing.

At first, he thought it was his brain playing tricks on him.
But they were happy tricks. And it was an unbelievably
hard time. Charlie Sr had lost his beloved grandson but
that paled at the pain of watching his daughter grieve for
her son. Charlie Sr had never seen anyone in so much pain,
and there was nothing he could do for her. He just had to
wait for her heart to grow to accommodate all that grief. So
if he spent the evening playing pairs or solitaire with his
grandson, where was the harm?

The years passed, and his daughter was starting to seem

human again. She was still frail. Her hair was thinner, her skin didn't glow. But she could get around the grocery store without crying at Charlie Jr's favourite yoghurt. She could sit through a family dinner. Her friends (those that stuck with her, of which there were few) could even persuade her to go out for coffee, instead of staying at home.

She was learning to live with the grief. But Charlie Sr was still playing cards with his grandson's ghost every night. So he decided to go to the Doctor. He was not completely honest. He didn't use the word ghost, even though he was sure that was what he was seeing. He talked about seeing things, perhaps out the corner of his eye. The Doctor spoke calmly, checking the visions didn't upset Charlie Sr, or say anything scary. She suggested an eye test first. Then, if his sight was okay they could think about more tests. She spoke a lot about loneliness and gave him leaflets from Age UK and Men's Shed, where he could spend Thursday afternoons with other older men repairing things or building picnic benches for the park.

Charlie Sr went and had his eyes tested. Except for a little shadow that would probably become a cataract in a year or two, his eyes were fine. He didn't return to the Doctor. The Doctor hadn't seemed too alarmed, hadn't rushed him in for a brain scan. The Doctor obviously thought it was loneliness, not anything scary. And Charlie Sr didn't feel lonely. So he kept playing cards with the ghost of Charlie Jr.

But as the years passed, Charlie Jr was becoming bored of playing cards. There is only so much you can do with a ghost. Charlie Jr couldn't touch anything, so they couldn't play computer games. Charlie Jr still kept bugging his grandad to get one. He wanted to know what it was like, these new games that he saw advertised on TV. Charlie Jr had died before home computers were common. Now boys had their own games consoles.

Charlie Sr gave in and bought one. He told his daughter he wanted to keep his brain and coordination sharp in his retirement. He learnt to play Grand Theft Auto. He wasn't sure it was suitable for his 7 year old grandson. But Charlie Jr had been 7 a very long time and had been through some truly scary experiences at the hospital. And he didn't seem to sleep, so the game wasn't going to give him nightmares.

But of course, Charlie Jr soon got frustrated with the game. Charlie Sr wasn't pressing the right buttons fast enough. And Charlie Jr couldn't press them at all. They tried crosswords, but Charlie Jr hadn't grown old enough to learn to spell, nor experienced enough to untangle the clues. They tried reading and watching movies but Charlie Jr got bored and restless. Yet he couldn't tell his grandfather what he wanted.

Charlie Sr started to wonder what it was holding Charlie Jr's ghost here. He was the only ghost Charlie Sr had ever seen. But, as a sociologist, he couldn't believe that this was a phenomenon just for him. There had to be a pattern. So Charlie started to attend bereavement groups. He thought perhaps he could find someone else who had a ghost. And then they could talk about how to keep them entertained.

In the end, the answer came a little closer to home. Charlie Sr was weeding his garden one day. Charlie Jr was with him but was bored by the activity. The neighbour Yvonne came down the garden with a cup of coffee. Charlie Sr said good morning, and Charlie Jr gasped. Charlie Jr could see the ghost of an old woman just behind Yvonne.

The four of them sat down to coffee. It was a stilted conversation. Charlie Jr, and the other ghost (Mrs Thomas) could see each other. But Charlie Sr and Yvonne could only see their own ghosts. The novelty wore off quickly for Charlie Jr. Even though he was a ghost, he was still a 7 year old boy. And coffee in the garden was boring. Until Yvonne mentioned that her mother had seen a ghost.

'She used to tell us about the ghost of her sister. No-one else ever saw this ghost. And mum didn't seem that bothered by it. I didn't believe it was really a ghost. But it seemed to keep mum happy.' Yvonne dissolved into tears and looked guiltily over her shoulder at the ghost of her mum.

'The trouble is mum lived alone. Like you,' she nodded at Charlie Sr. 'It's so difficult, when Robert gets in from work. He tries to be sympathetic. But mum wants to keep watching her soaps. And Robert thinks it's unhealthy that I've suddenly become obsessed with watching all the shows mum used to love. Mum says I should just tell him the truth but I'm not sure that will help. Robert is a very practical person.'

Charlie Sr nodded and sympathised, but couldn't suggest anything helpful. Yvonne had been wondering if it wouldn't last too long, and perhaps the ghost would go before Robert had enough and moved out. But Charlie Jr being there 30 years after his death put paid to that hope. Charlie Sr asked how long her mother saw her sister's ghost. Yvonne looked surprised and shrugged. She looked over her shoulder.

'14 years,' she replied, repeating what her ghost was telling her for the benefit of Charlie Sr.

'But mum hasn't seen her since the day she died.'

This made sense to Charlie Sr, in a way. If we were going to accept the presence of ghosts, then how is the world not overrun with them? The idea of one in, one out makes sense. Perhaps the person you were thinking of as you died. Some people weren't thinking of anyone, so didn't become a ghost. Or were thinking of people already dead. Charlie Sr was kind of touched that Charlie Jr had been thinking of him. And glad that Charlie Jr hadn't thought of his mother. Charlie Sr wasn't sure his daughter would have survived seeing a ghost. The theory took shape in Charlie Sr's head, and although he didn't write it down, he enjoyed working it through as if it were a paper he was going to present.

The idea had obviously stuck with Charlie Jr too. He realised that the only way anything would change for him, was for his grandpa to die. He didn't want him dead, but it probably was his turn. Charlie Sr would just have to be very careful about his thoughts in his final moments.

Charlie Sr agreed that part world be easy. He would think of his wife, who had died before Charlie Jr got sick. She lived long enough to meet her grandson, to buy Christmas presents and throw birthday teas. But not long enough to have to sit by the phone during hospital appointments.

But, while Charlie Sr has always said that he would do anything for his children, he wasn't sure about this. He had often prayed while Charlie Jr was in the hospital, offering himself as a trade. He wasn't particularly religious and felt that he was praying to the universe rather than a specific God. But it hadn't worked anyway. Now he had the chance to make that trade, and he hesitated.

Charlie Sr pondered over his hesitation, trying to uncover the root of it. He finally thought back to that Doctor's appointment. One of the questions she had asked was whether the visions ever made him feel bad, or scared, or wanted him to hurt himself. He'd answered no at the time of course. But perhaps that was why he was holding back. What if the ghost of Charlie Jr wasn't real?

Charlie Sr decided it was time to write a paper. The experience he had of his ghost. He interviewed Yvonne the neighbour, and, by proxy of course, her mother. He tried to find online sources, but there was too much nonsense to try and get through to actually find reliable accounts. He could go back to the grief groups. But Charlie Jr was starting to get impatient. He had been 7 a very long time. He was ready for the next step, whatever that might be.

So Charlie Sr has a decision to make. He could believe his own experience. He could believe in the sixth sense of the universe, that kept some people from boarding planes. Or he could go back to the Doctor, for more tests, medication and procedures. He began making plans. He tidied out his shed and organised the attic. He made sure all his bills were well organised and created a ring-binder labelled "important" with a copy of each utility bill and a bank statement.

At the end, it wasn't a hard choice. He stayed awake late that night, thinking it over, making sure he hadn't missed anything. He didn't write a note to his daughter, because there was nothing left to say. It was just time. He sat sipping tea and taking a mixture of pills he had collected. He slipped away just before dawn, thinking of his wife and grandson.

Night and Day

by Brad Petrie

Bradley Petrie is a final year student at Bournemouth University. Throughout his degree, he has been able to write two short pieces of fiction which he is very proud of. After hearing about the Bournemouth Writing Prize for his final writing assignment, he was excited to submit them and enter the competition himself in hopes of his work being recognised professionally.

I will never forget the night I first heard it. A delicate harmony whispered through the air from afar. It was like nothing I'd ever heard before. The sound kissed the breeze and brought a warmth that alleviated the bitterness of the night. A song sweeter than the birds. Clearer than a waterfall.

When I was young my parents and I were travellers. We lived in a small carriage which we'd move from town to town, only traveling at night. We never stayed anywhere too long before we had to pack what we had and be back on the road. I was never schooled but they made sure I could read and write. They taught me to never go out during the day. Daylight is poisonous, strictly move in the dark. So that's what we did. I can't recall on many memories from my childhood, it feels like an eternity ago. A distant memory that fades ever more each day. I was 18 when I last saw them both. We were staying in a cave in a remote hillside surrounded by enormous ancient trees and crashing waterfalls. We'd never stayed this far out before. I rose in our cave in time with the moon like we always did but my parents were nowhere to be seen. The carriage was gone too with no explanation. I haven't seen them since. Why would they leave me here? Time moves fast when you live alone in the wild, I'm not sure how long it's been since the day they left, so long I lost count of my age too. It can be lonely at times, even the animals run from me. When the moon comes out and I awake, they hide underground or in the trees out of sight. Sometimes I worry my parents felt the same as the animals and I scared them away.

There was nothing unusual about the night I heard it. I awoke from the same cave in the hillside as the poisonous sun went down and the moon was high in the sky. The cold thin air seeped through skin and rattled my bones. The small scurry of mice or flapping of wings in the trees above was heightened tonight. After sleeping for what felt like a few moons, a supernatural urge takes over your body, pushing you in the direction of food. My throat gasping for any drop of blood I could get my hands on. Now I understand the poor animals fear. My parents would always catch their food and leave me the blood because they knew it was my favourite. That night an unsuspecting deer was drinking from the river at the nearest waterfall. They didn't finish a sip before I sunk my teeth into its warm neck. It squealed and jittered in the running water before giving in to its inevitable end. The remains were dragged back to my cave where it will lay on the cold wet floor before my next feed. An overwhelming sense of guilt overcame me after every feed, with the little memory I had, I could never recall my parents letting me feed this much. As I've gotten older, I crave animals' blood more and more. The guilt of them seeing me now always brings me to the one spot I feel comfortable.

Beyond the waterfalls and away from my cave there was a hill. This hill was the highest point for as far as the eye could see. The view from here was remarkable, you could see the icy wind flowing through the dips in the land, rustling even the highest leaves in the tallest trees. Beautiful deep-yellow flowers scattered across the grass all the way up the hill and at the very peak lived a single apple tree. Its blood-red fruit lay around its base and across the grass which mingled with the flowers to create a collage of colour. I found comfort in this tree; we have a lot in common. All alone in a land we didn't choose to live. Then I heard it.

It broke the deafening silence and rolled gently up the hill where I lay. For a second, I felt hypnotised, the cold left my body like I'd been gifted a hug from an angel. As an apple fell from the tree I jumped to my feet and scanned the land beneath me, a beaming light came from a small shack amongst the forest on the opposite side of the hill. This wasn't here before. How long did I sleep this time? Recently the concept of time has been fading quickly, I couldn't keep track of how many moons had passed since I last left my cave but other than my parents, I had never seen another person here before. Could it be them? Then I saw long blonde hair belonging to the angel draping out of the window and blew softly in the wind. We seemed to be a similar age. Her skin as golden as her hair, it reminded me of my mother's. My pale veiny skin was always different but it never seemed this cold and empty. She sat dreamily on the window ledge and hummed mystical spells into what looked like a violin. I'd read about them but never seen or heard one before. I sat and watched until the night began to retire, a slither of sunlight peeked over the horizon and singed my skin back to reality. Who was this girl?

I came back for the next three moons in awe of this girl trying to work out who she was and how she made such mesmerising songs. That was until one night just before the sun rose, the girl looked up at the single tree on the tallest hill and caught me gazing. We stared at each other for a moment, her river-water-blue eyes fixated on mine. For the first time in forever I felt like the thing looking back wasn't scared of me. She darted from the window and I scurried like a mouse behind the apple tree. Peering between the branches at the shack I saw the girl stood between two men, much bigger than her. The men came out wielding arrows and spears.

'Are you sure you saw it?' the burly men asked hurryingly. The girl paused for a second, looked back up at the tree, fixated again.

'No,' she lied without taking her eyes from the hill.

'What have we told you about going outside at night,

it's dangerous, now come inside,' the tallest of the two demanded.

'The night? Dangerous?' I murmured to myself puzzlingly. The light where the girl sat went out and I retreated back to my cave.

*

It must have been many moons before I went back to the hill. I was still shaken by the men who protected the girl. As I climbed up the great hill, I noticed some of the apples fallen from the tree had been eaten. I looked around for more clues until I came across something sticky lodged in the roots of the trees. It was a violin, the same violin the girl had been playing. I picked it up and began to play. A harsh screech echoed through the valley. With that, the girl's light flickered and there she was, holding a violin of her own. She looked up at me with a smile and began playing. This girl was truly an angel. I came back to the hill every night to watch the girl play. The more I watched, the more I fell for her. We lived such different lives, but we had made a connection through music. I practised and practised in hopes that one day we could play together. The girl could only go out during the day when the blistering sun was high in the sky, she was otherworldly but to me she was perfect.

Every so often the girl would leave me letters to read when I got to the hill. Her name was Rose. She told me all about her days when I wasn't around and left drawings of the two of us playing our violins together. She explained how her brothers would not let her out at night as there were deadly creatures that lurked in the forest. I wrote back to tell her I'd never seen these deadly creatures and that her brothers were wrong. We wrote letters and played our violins from afar every night, as the moons went by. I got better and better at the violin but never as good as Rose. I could never get bored of watching her play, each night was as beautiful as the first. I never wanted it to end. The cursing crack of sunlight in the horizon forced me to leave the hill and away from Rose, if only she would see there were no creatures out here. I have never hated the sun more than now; it was the only thing stopping us from being together. While I hid from its rays back in my cave, Rose clouded my mind. The sweet sound of her music played on repeat in my head. I imagined how her golden hair would feel between my fingers, seeing her baby blue eyes flickering in the light instead of the pitch black. That was until one night, she left another note. 'In three nights, time, meet here, love Rose x'. Could this be a trick I wondered? Could her brothers be trying to lure me into a trap? I waited for her to appear but for the first time, she never came. The light in her shack never flickered and her music never played.

'Three nights time,' I muttered. 'Three nights time.' On the third moon I decided to make my way to the hill, I had to be cautious this time, it could be a trap after all. As I slowly climbed, I could hear that unmistakable sound coming from the top of the hill. Then I saw her. Elegantly sat at the base of the tree, her pearl white dress and wavy hair blew in the wind. I moved closer until we sat side by side.

You're not that scary for a vampire,' she said.

Fox Night

by Leigh Rocha

Leigh Rocha lives with her family in a ramshackle old house, overlooking the sea. Her guiltiest pleasure is to peer in and out; looking for the tales you find where ancient and present co-exist. She is moved by the magic that shifts beneath the beech trees and the healing that is to be found as you look out to hill and harbour. She loves to listen to the stories that drift in with the Spring hawthorn, run with the Autumn squirrels and dance around the house; shaping her rhythm.

Did she really want to take herself back? Push and claw through time; batting it all out the way until she was there. She had often wondered if this was where it would all end, but for the longest time she refused to go; stubbornly, lips pursed. Of course, deep down she knew that it was inevitable; that it would worm its way in, take her unawares, force her to remember.

I'm growing old and I wanna go home.

Really? Home? Home to Salterns?

She steeled herself for the pain and was surprised to hear instead a little gasp of longing. So, this really was the time to go home after all. She reached deep inside herself and fumbled for the silver pin. So tiny. So hidden. Once in her hands she had to turn it. Before she heard the gentle click of the lock, she realised exactly where it would take her, and she wept. She was nearly there; so close now, feet on gravel, running harder and faster, lungs full of green, past the storm-purple of the rhododendrons, brushing past the house, across the moon-lit lawn rolling off towards the sea and falling to her knees beneath the beeches. The lock was turned. The lid of her little gold box sprung open, and she peered inside.

She was back.

Back to the March-Moon night. Back to long silver shadows. Back to the dance of his tiny birdy-beat. Back to Fox Night.

And she was surprised. It hadn't entered her head that this was what she would find. But finding herself here she felt the weight of her empty arms. She felt the weight of her cow heavy body; skin puckered and tight, hot and milky. She braced herself for what she thought would come first.

She knew it had the power to consume her – to set her loose into the void – to throw her to the black-eyed dog. She knew well enough to bend to it, to bow down to it, to ride the wave, to let it drain the blood from her, to tighten its grip on her, to feel herself teeter on the very, very edge. White knuckles. Empty. Un-woman. Shell. Pull your socks up stupid girl. But that wasn't what she saw when she peered deep inside. It was him.

*

Him who smelt of the woodshed, who took her hand, who it turned out, had known the answer all along. And she smiled despite when they were. And she let him take her to the bench where she tucked her legs beneath herself and bathed in the heat from their fire. Let the silence between tell everything.

She yearned for nothing.

Here on Fox Night, she held his hand safe in the hold of the whispering trees. She held his hand and saw them from afar, as they must have seemed from the house; two heads together, silhouetted against the rising haze of their fire as each spark shot stars into space. She held his hand and waited for the foxes.

There, beneath the beeches, she crouched with them and the rhythm grew beneath her from deep within the earth, until her whole being danced with it. The moon sailed silently across the sky, each wax and wane marking her time. She felt her breath rise up and off into the night, felt it fill the space between beginning and end. She looked back one last time, over her shoulder at home. Home, who shone in the moonlight. Home, whose eyes looked out over the beeches to the moon-drenched sea. She lowered her gaze in thanks and closed the lid on her little gold box.

The Lake at the Bottom of the Garden
by John Ward

John is a member of Watford Writers. However, they have recently moved from Watford to Bournemouth. John has written 120 short stories, 90 poems, three plays, three monologues and a Pantomime.

It was to be my parents dream house, they said. I was no more than seven years old when we moved in, an exciting time for my mother and father who had worked hard to build up their retail business to afford their new home in this expensive area of Surrey.

Unfortunately, this left little time in their lives for their only son, me. The features of the house they liked best were the gardens. We had never had a garden before, so we were going to enjoy this new aspect. That was the original plan. It never quite worked out like that. My parent's business was still expanding and they never had the time to spend planting, picking, cultivating and maintaining the plant life. They hired gardeners to keep it looking good.I was an only child and when I was young my parents hired a nanny to look after me during the day and sometimes in the evening too. As the nanny spent most of each day cuddling a bottle of alcohol, I was left, by and large, to my own devices.

I therefore had plenty of time to search and investigate the gardens. There were three distinct areas: the formal gardens near the house, the orchard, and the lake at the bottom of the garden. Although I could go to all these areas, I kept to the areas near the house. The upper garden could be compared to a typical garden in suburbia, laid out with shrubs and flowers and trees, with a working vegetable and herb garden. Ours was much bigger than the usual suburban garden, of course, but similar if one ignored the ornamental fountain and the sculptures and topiary strategically placed for maximum visual effect. It had been designed by one of the foremost landscape gardeners of the day for the previous occupant of the house, a guitarist for a world-renowned rock band. As he travelled the world with his band I doubt that he spent much time there either. When the band was about to reach the peak of their fame, the guitarist disappeared, presumed by the rest of the band to have joined a religious cult in America. The house had lain empty for more than a year when it became ours.

The upper garden needed some serious attention to bring it back to its former glory. The meadow needed a week of scythes and mowers. The workers did not venture near the lake.

I played the normal boy's games among the rockeries, war games with model army characters. Sometimes, one or two boys my age would come to play. They were from the local village but I wouldn't call them friends. Each one drifted away in short time. Either they didn't like me, nor my nanny shouting at them from the house, or they were suspicious of the atmosphere surrounding the area of the lake.

Over a period of time, I became more solitary and no one would come to visit me. I preferred to keep to the upper garden. At the furthermost part of the upper garden there was a brick wall with an attractive arch and a metal gate. This led through to the second section, the orchard and meadow. I kept away from this archway. I could not explain why; it was just an uneasy feeling, my chest was tighter, my pulse rate increasing. Don't get me wrong, I love gardens in general. I preferred to keep to the upper garden where I felt safe, away from the spirits, but occasionally I was inexplicably drawn through the arched gate.

Beyond the wall was the meadow and orchard. Despite the huge volume of apples produced by the orchard, the temperature always dropped several degrees once stepping through the gate, as though the gate itself was a portal to a more sinister world. There was no obvious reason and all the head gardeners and nurserymen with whom my parents had discussed this phenomenon were baffled.

I knew, of course. It was the influence of the lower garden.

As I grew into my teenage years, I ventured more often into the orchard, but not through choice. I was being drawn through the gate. I would tell myself that I was going in for the apples. Sometimes they would be sweet, sometimes bitter. When sweet, I would collect some and take them back to the house. When bitter, I could feel icy fingers drawing me onwards, beckoning me to the lower garden. It was hard to resist and sometimes I couldn't. I would come out of that stagnant area an hour later, shivering, cold, and babbling, unable to say what had happened there. Not because I didn't want to, it was because I didn't know. The lower part of the garden was always a mystery to me; sometimes benign, occasionally beautiful, but often terrifying. From an early age it scared me even to think of it. I fantasised about it during the days and I had nightmares about it at night. I avoided it because I believed the evil spirits lived there, waiting to claim me.

Let me tell you about that garden.

It was always dark. No sun rays ever penetrated the thick foliage. The central feature was a fetid lake in which the water was black and never moved, a scum sitting on the top. No wildlife went near it; no fish, no birds, no frogs, no dragonflies. Nothing. It was black, silent and still. Dark trees would overhang but where branches touched the water the tree would seem to be dying upwards from that point, the leaves curling up like arthritic hands before dropping dead.

A fence made from wooden stakes encircled the lake, each stake bound to its neighbour with thick entwined wire running alongside a narrow uneven path of earth, with long tree roots bursting through that made walking treacherous. The roots seemed to grab at my ankles as I moved past them. The lake was surrounded by dense foliage, thick shrubs and trees intertwined. Nothing bloomed there except a large, dark maroon flower which would appear and disappear within two days.

The smell of rotting vegetation stung the inside of the nostrils and made my eyes weep. If a droplet of water fell off a leaf and touched bare skin it would be as if a needle had been stuck into me.

I tried calling out, even shouting, to check if my voice would carry, but any cry was immediately enveloped by the foliage as if the noise was encircled and gathered in, thus stopping any sound escaping from that evil place.

At one time my father hired someone to clear the lake. The man went into the lower garden to see what the job entailed but came out within five minutes to tell my father he wouldn't do it. My father persuaded him to take on the job by the offer of three times the going rate. He came back the next day, entered the garden, and we never saw him again. We tried to convince ourselves that he had changed his mind and didn't want to tell us, but I know it was the spirits that carried him down to the depths of the lake. My family never mentioned him again.

As I reached adulthood, my mother passed away and my father became more irritable and set in his ways. We would disagree on many things and have raging arguments. I became more insular and spent more and more time in that evil place. I came to love it instead of hating it but I was still fearful. It had me in its power. When I came out of that garden, I could never remember what I'd done, even though I may have been there several hours. My father thought I was on drugs. He was right, I was, but that was not the cause of my paranoia, it was just a symptom. I needed the drugs just to find the courage to be there. My father never entered that part of the garden, not until that fateful day. We had an argument in the house and, as usual, I headed for the garden. This time he followed me, shouting.

As I entered the area of the lake, I heard the trees rustle. This had not happened before. The spirits did not like the angry words. By this time the spirits and I were one. They wanted to protect me. I turned to warn my father of the danger but as I looked the tree roots rose around his legs tripping him. Wet, long creepers rose out of the lake, encircled his body and in a moment dragged him in. He disappeared beneath the surface before he could call out or I could move to help him. The lake was still again, as if nothing had happened.

Blood Ties

By Ekaterina Crawford

Ekaterina was born and grew up in Moscow and now lives in Aldershot with her husband and their two children. She always loved writing but it's only in the past few years that she really pursued her passion.

Ekaterina's creative pieces were published by the Visual Verse Anthology. She has won Writers' Forum Magazine Poetry Competition and was placed third in their short stories Competition. She has also won 2021 Kingston Libraries Short Stories Competition.

In anticipation of the afternoon show, the crowds in Kentish Town had already begun to flock towards the concert hall.

'How could you do this to me, David?' Pacing the alley behind the Forum, Liz shouted into her phone. 'No! I don't need another excuse. No! I don't want to know! Allow me to remind you that it was you who begged me to give us another chance. And now another no-show? I can't do this anymore, David. It's over!'

She hung up but a few moments later she dialled back.

'And get your stuff out of my flat! Tomorrow! I have a session in the gym after lunch. Come then. I don't want to see your face ever again!'

Pushing through the concert crowd towards the station, she collided with a tall handsome man dressed way too elegantly for a rock concert. Cursing under her breath, she shot an angry glance at the man, who, stretching his lips in a most charming of smiles, saluted an apology with his umbrella and disappeared into the sea of faces.

Kentish Town station was closed. The white board outside spoke of an earlier passenger incident and members of transport police guided stressed travellers towards the nearest bus stops.

The afternoon was warm. Feeling the need for a dose of fresh air, Liz strolled through Camden and entered Regent's Park via Gloucester Gate.

Reaching the boating lake, she flopped onto the first bench, stretched out her tired legs and began working through her social media accounts, deleting all the evidence of her relationship with David. When she wiped off the last post and changed her relationship status to single, she looked up and saw the familiar four- legged creature trotting towards her from the side the boathouse. The husky dog approached her violently wagging his tail. 'Look who's here! Hey, buddy!' She scanned the surroundings for the dog's owner. 'Did you run away again?'

The husky danced around her, squealing in excitement.

'Oh, I missed you too!' she laughed, ruffling the dog's thick fur. 'Why can't David be like you? Devoted and loyal?' The dog whined in reply, looking at her with his astonishingly blue eyes. 'Actually, when I think about it, you're kind of the same – both leave me and then both come back when I least expect it. Bad boys! Well, never mind. Come.'

She patted the bench. The dog jumped and curled up next to her, placing his heavy head onto her lap. The husky closed his eyes and lay, not moving, responding to Liz's hand running through his fur with a sound of pure joy, while she, oblivious to what was happening around her, scrolled through the latest headlines.

Gothic nightmare descends upon London.

Blood-drained body found in North-West London

'Jeez,' she muttered, gently pulling at the husky's ear. 'What is it? The Duke fucking Dracula on the loose?'

'Count,' came from her left.

Liz yelped. Immediately alert, the husky jumped to his feet and growled.

On the bench next to them, sat a young man dressed in a navy-blue suit and tailored black overcoat with a delicate brooch pinned to the lapel. Waves of his dark hair nestled comfortably upon his shoulders. His angular profile was clean and sharp, if a little pale. His strong chin and high cheekbones, together with the slightly elongated nose, seemed strangely elegant and aristocratic. His eyes were hidden behind designer sunglasses. In his hands, he held a black stick umbrella.

Liz stared, restraining the husky with both hands.

'I'm sorry,' the stranger said, removing his shades. His

deep hazelnut eyes gleamed like a liquid gold. 'I didn't mean to startle you. I merely wanted to point out that Dracula was a Count, not a Duke.'

'What? Who cares?' she blurted out. 'Dracula's just a character in a book.'

The stranger smiled, exposing even white teeth.

'Let's leave it to the historians and literati to argue whether Bram Stoker's dramatisation was based on a real person or a fictional character,' he said. Words rolled out of his mouth like water in a stream, soft and smooth. 'Better tell me, what a beautiful lady like you is doing here alone?'

'Can't see how it's any of your business,' Liz retorted, carefully eyeing the stranger. 'Do I know you?'

'My apologies. I didn't mean to pry,' the stranger slightly nodded his head, 'and to answer your question: Yes. We have met. You bumped into me. Earlier today.'

'What?' Liz's hands went limp.

The husky growled, sniffed the stranger, growled again, and climbed onto the bench between them. Leaning against Liz, he pushed the man towards the edge of his seat.

'H-Have you been following me?' Liz glanced around.

'Nothing sinister. I assure you. When I saw you earlier today you seemed...somewhat upset. I simply wanted to make sure you were all right.'

'Oh.' She blushed.

Immune to the stranger's charms, the dog rolled onto its side and pushed harder against the man's leg and then, with his lips stretched and tongue out, looked up at Liz for approval.

'I didn't know people still did that,' she blushed again and patted the husky's belly.

'Did what?' The stranger smiled, amused by the dog's desperate efforts to push him off the bench.

'Cared for what's happening around them.'

'Seemed natural.'

'Not in Central London. Most would've just walked past.'

'I'm glad I didn't.'

He smiled, placed the umbrella on his lap and leaned against the backrest of the bench. The tips of his fingers brushed against Liz's, leaving a hot tingling sensation on her skin. She found herself unable to move, unable to look away. The dog sat up and growled, baring his teeth in warning.

'Sorry,' Liz jerked her head. 'You were saying?'

'I don't think your dog particularly likes me,' the stranger laughed softly.

'He's not mine. He just hangs out with me sometimes. So I guess he feels protective?'

She pulled her hand away and glanced around.

'I'd better be going.'

She got up. The husky jumped off the bench and stood by her feet.

'Thank you for your concern. It was a pleasure to meet you...Tom.'

'Tom?' The stranger raised his perfectly-shaped eyebrow.

With her cheeks turning beetroot once again, Liz pointed at the name sticker attached to the umbrella.

'Oh! This little thing. I...borrowed it. From a person I knew. Allow me to introduce myself. Vladislav Konstantin Alexander Dragan.'

'European?' Liz stared. 'I would never have guessed! Your English is perfect. Where are you from? Italy? Spain?'

'Romania,' he smiled seductively. 'Your tabloids call me "the Romanian Prince".'

'Oh yes, I think I read it somewhere. Wait- Do you mean like a *prince* prince?'

'You could say that,' he smiled again. His eyes glowed softly, reflecting the light of the afternoon sun.

Liz no longer felt like going home. Strangely enough, she was even glad that David had stood her up.

'Elizabeth, Elizabeth Thornton,' she said and stretched out her hand, already imagining herself walking down the aisle of an ancient church with a diamond tiara on her head, and then riding off in a royal carriage. 'Friends call me Liz.'

'Pleasure to make your acquaintance, Miss Thornton,' he placed a gentle kiss on the back of her hand. 'You can call me Vlad. And now, if you'll allow me, I would like to escort you home. It's getting late.'

Vlad led her towards the gates. The husky trotted behind them, keeping a cautious eye on Liz's new acquaintance.

'So. How long are you in London for?' Liz asked as they reached the exit.

'For a couple of weeks,' Vlad said, effortlessly pulling the iron gates open.

'Are you on a royal tour or something?'

Vlad drew her arm through his and pointed his slender finger at the double-decker bus standing at the traffic light.

'"The Week of Romanian Culture in London,"' Liz read out loud. 'Right! That explains your reaction when I said Dracula was just a character in a book. He's a part of your country's history!'

Vlad's lips curled.

Behind them, the dog produced a sound transcending from a faint squeal into a low growl.

'So,' Liz prompted, glancing back at her four-legged companion. 'Was he real? The blood-sucking terror?'

'There are a few theories,' Vlad said as they reached the Landmark Hotel. 'We could have discussed it. Over dinner. But I already ate.'

'Yeah, I noticed that!' Liz giggled. 'I'm sorry, I should've said before. You have a little ketchup. There. Allow me.'

He caught her hand before it reached his face, his fingers locked around her wrist like an iron shackle, his hazelnut eyes turned black.

The husky barked. Vlad let go of her hand, pulled a handkerchief from his pocket and wiped the corners of his mouth.

'There,' he said, a familiar golden glow shining through his eyes once again. 'I didn't mean to scare you. It's just... you caught me in a very...um...un-prince-like moment. I apologise. Humbly. And to make it up to you, if you'll allow it, of course, I'd like to buy you a drink.'

In the Bell Inn, they ordered drinks and took a table by the back wall. Outside, the husky barked and squealed, begging to be let in. Each time the door opened, Liz stole a quick glance of the furry creature that sat patiently by the front door, sniffing each new visitor entering the pub.

'That dog seems very attached to you,' Vlad said, placing a bottle of tequila, saltshaker, and a plate with lemons on the table.

'He's been following me around for some months now. He comes and goes. I don't even know whose he is.'

'Well, doesn't matter.' Vlad poured out a shot of tequila and pushed it closer to Liz. 'Better tell me what made you so upset?'

'I had a fight with my boyfriend.' Liz downed the shot and bit into a lemon wedge. 'Ah, that's good! Not boyfriend, more of a fiancé really. Well, ex-fiancé turned boyfriend again, ex-boyfriend now...I guess.'

'Sounds complicated.' Vlad refilled her glass.

'Not really. Well, yes it was. In a way. Not anymore.'

'I'm sorry to hear it.'

His hand covered hers; the light tingling sensation spread over her skin.

'It's all right. It was long coming. We drifted apart about

a year ago. He asked me to give it another chance. I made an effort. He made promises...You know how it is.'

'I'm afraid I don't,' Vlad shook his head. 'I would never have betrayed my word to such a beautiful lady like yourself.'

Liz smiled, drowning in his dark eyes.

'You know what?' she said after downing another shot. 'It's getting late, and I was thinking, do you, maybe, want to come over to my place? I live just around the corner. We can have a quiet drink. Or two. Get to know each other a little better.'

'You just broke up with your boyfriend. I don't want—' his fingers caressed her cheek.

'Don't worry, you won't take advantage of my broken heart. Whatever happens, happens. No strings attached.'

'If you insist.' He leaned in, his cold lips brushed lightly against hers. 'Just give me a minute.'

Vlad got up and strolled off towards the toilets.

With nothing else to do, Liz turned her attention to the news feed on the large TV that hung behind the bar. The screen showed a police cordon and a coroner's van. The breaking news message at the bottom of the screen read:

The body found earlier today in Kentish Town has now been officially identified as 29-year-old Tom Mitchel from Hampstead Heath. Police appealing for any witnesses.

Liz stared at the TV screen, then at the umbrella perched against the wall, then at the screen again, and then at the untouched glass of red wine on the table in front of her.

The vision of her royal wedding faded away, replaced by the sight of a police cordon and a coroner's van.

Immediately sober, she grabbed her bag and rushed out of the pub. Hiding behind the delivery van and keeping her eyes on the front door, she slowly backed off until she slipped and landed into the puddle of dark sticky substance next to the bloodless corpse dressed in the UPS uniform.

Slipping and slithering, she scrambled up to her feet and dashed to the other side of the deserted street. She ran into the churchyard and hid behind a headstone. The full moon shed its cold silver onto the graves. Somewhere in the distance, a dog howled.

'You can run, but you can't hide,' Vlad's deep voice came from the other side of the churchyard.

Covering her mouth with both hands, Liz froze. She closed her eyes, trying to blend into the headstone. Blood throbbed in her temples, echoing approaching steps.

'Hello, beautiful,' Vlad whispered into her ear.

She spun around, her horrified eyes met his black stare.

'Now. How about that drink?' he smiled, his canine teeth grew longer.

An ear-piercing scream ripped through the air. She couldn't recognise her own voice. Vlad yanked her up as if she was no heavier than a rag doll and threw her to the other side of the yard.

Liz landed hard, hitting her face against the stone wall. Her vision began to blur, surroundings slowly fading away. Now it was only her and a slowly approaching dark shadow. Its sinister laugh rang in her ears.

She opened her eyes. Vlad's white, luminous skin looked almost transparent against the backdrop of the night sky. His cold fingers touched the cut on her face.

'It would be a pity to kill you,' he said licking the blood off his fingers. 'But you're so delicious.'

Vlad grabbed the sides of her jacket, pinned her against the wall and drew back the collar of her blouse, exposing her jugular vein.

'Goodbye, Liz Thornton. It was a pleasure to make your acquaintance.'

Resigned to her fate, Liz went limp in his hands. But just

before the sharp teeth sunk into her skin, she saw a flash of silver fur as the husky charged at the vampire, pushing it away.

The dog stood between her and Vlad. Then with a menacing growl, he launched forward, knocking the vampire off its feet. The churchyard became loud with heavy grunts and barks. The two predators growled and snarled, snapping their teeth, trying to get a taste of each other's flesh.

The husky was the first to succeed. Vlad roared in pain, shook the dog off his leg, and kicked it hard, sending it flying to the other side of the yard. With a cry of pain, the dog crashed into a gravestone. Then everything went quiet. The vampire vanished, leaving its prey behind.

Liz found the husky by one of the graves. He was lying still, his belly rising and falling with each laboured breath.

'Come on, buddy,' she sobbed, stroking his fur. 'Get up. Please.'

The dog opened his eyes, pressed his nose against her hand, and closed them again. On his head, just above his eye, a deep wound oozed blood.

Liz carefully heaved the dog off the ground and carried it to her apartment.

After attending to the Husky's wounds, she left him on the couch. She showered, changed into a clean tracksuit, and made herself strong coffee with a shot of whisky. Curled on the sofa next to her four-legged saviour, she stared at the large silver disk of the moon that hung outside her window.

The next morning, she woke up in her own bed.

Staggering into the empty lounge, she heaved herself onto the sofa and clasped her head between her palms, trying to silence the toll of the hangover bells. Did she dream it all? Vampires? Dead bodies? A nearly finished bottle of whisky on the floor by the couch confirmed her suspicions.

Wrapped in the duvet, ready to give in to a hungover slumber, she heard the sound of a boiling kettle, which was followed by the smell of freshly brewed coffee coming from the kitchen.

'David?' Liz scrambled up to her feet, and with a duvet still upon her head, waddled into the kitchen. 'What the fuck, David? I thought I told you I don't want to...'

She froze in the doorway. David stood by the table. His shirt was undone, revealing a huge bruise on the left side of his torso. There were a few small scratches across his face and a deep cut on the left side of his temple, just above his eye.

'Morning love,' he smiled, his astonishingly blue eyes gleamed in the light of the morning sun. 'Thank you for looking after me yesterday. I hope that bloodsucker didn't scare you too much. Coffee?'

'You?' Liz muttered, the duvet slowly sliding onto the floor. 'You! It was you all the time!'

She took a cautious step closer and ran her fingers over the scarring skin above his eye. David drew back.

'Careful, love. I heal fast, but it still hurts like hell.'

'W-why didn't you tell me?'

'Would you have believed me if I did?' he smiled.

'No way!' she brushed off approaching tears and buried her face into his chest. 'Though it does explain why you've refused to adopt a cat.'

David chuckled, placing a soft kiss upon her head. 'I always told you, I'm more of a dog person.'

The Bournemouth Writing Prize 2022 invites you to

COLLECT THEM ALL!

Four more astonishing anthologies from this year's competition.
All available to buy from Amazon.

Imprint

Pick Me Up

Dark Circles

Passages

Strange Encounters

BWP 2022

Make sure to tick off all five anthologies from this year's BWP! From fabulous female writers to feel good fiction, jaw dropping journeys to thunderous thrillers, you'll be amazed at what you find hidden in these pages!

☐ Imprint

☐ Pick Me Up

☐ Dark Circles

☐ Passages

☑ Strange Encounters

Printed in Great Britain
by Amazon